Totally Five Star: Monaco

BREAKING ROSSI'S RULES

KAIT GAMBLE

Breaking Rossi's Rules
ISBN # 978-1-78430-714-1
©Copyright Kait Gamble 2015
Cover Art by Posh Gosh ©Copyright August 2015
Interior text design by Claire Siemaszkiewicz
Totally Bound Publishing

Published in 2015 by Totally Bound Publishing, Newland House, The Point, Weaver Road, Lincoln, LN6 3QN, United Kingdom.

Totally Bound Publishing is a subsidiary of Totally Entwined Group Limited.

Totally Bound Publishing books by Kait Gamble:

The Long Way Round
Grind
Ignite

Totally Five Star
Breaking Rossi's Rules

BREAKING
ROSSI'S RULES

Dedication

For Faith

Chapter One

"Ms. De Winter! Ms. De Winter!"

Anika could hear the vultures through the tinted windows of the limo. Couldn't they just back off for a second? There had to be other news out there — besides her being left at the altar. Wasn't there some war going on? A banker caught embezzling? Surely, there was something more newsworthy than her life, or lack thereof, to report on.

"Ms. De Winter!" The horn-rimmed glasses and pink hair gave away the identity of the short woman grinning inanely in the front with her phone pointed directly at her. The blogger was like a piranha. And for some reason, she always focused on Anika. What was it she called herself again? Pink Penn? Pink Poison more like. The name was fitting.

"Is it true that he wasn't able to thaw the heart of the Ice Princess?"

It had been three days since she walked out of her own wedding, husbandless. What she hadn't realized until she'd gotten through the gauntlet of media and into her apartment in the trendiest part of London was that she wasn't at all upset. In fact, she felt free. The wedding, the preparations and the lies that surrounded it all had been wearing on her. It was so much fuss over something that was little more than a merger.

The paperwork that had been dispassionately signed by herself and her fiancé, Joshua Rhys-Jones, not two days before, delineated the fact in precise terms. Their families had been rivals for years but with the economy tanking, their fathers had the genius idea of merging their dwindling fortunes. It was an asinine idea, but there wasn't a thing they could do to go against the wishes of their families.

Joshua wasn't ugly by any means. He was well educated, looked good on her arm, and by all measures a stellar catch. She just didn't feel anything for him besides appreciation for her family's sake. He had admitted he felt the same. There was nothing romantic between them whatsoever, but they would make it appear how they wanted for the cameras just like they had been doing for the entirety of their lives.

So when he hadn't shown up for their wedding, she'd felt a myriad of emotions, though none of them had been sadness or shame. But whatever it was she felt was overridden by relief. It did, however, leave her confused and struggling to find the façade to use. When faced with the swarms of reporters and their questions, she didn't know what to do or how to act. It was just better to stay away from them.

"Drive on!" Anika didn't know what possessed her to think that it was okay to leave the apartment. No matter when she did, they were there ready to jump in her face. "Take me back home."

The car immediately started a slow roll through the throng and into the treacle-like traffic. What she wouldn't give to make it all go away.

Her phone trilled from inside her handbag, drawing her out of her misery. She extracted it and saw the familiar name. She swiped the screen. "Petra, you have to save me."

The voice on the other end burst into laughter. "Down in the doldrums, are you, darling? And after all the excitement?"

"You have no idea. The vultures won't leave me alone. No matter where I go, what I want to do, they're always in my face asking ridiculous questions. And why? Who cares? Why do they give a fig about my life?"

"Because the common people are enamored by the life of the rich and famous — especially when it crashes and burns. That's when they like to point and stare. It's the same logic as people who have to slow down and look at a car wreck."

Anika sighed. "So now you're comparing my life to a car wreck."

"Darling, if I didn't tell you, who would?"

Anika laughed for what felt like the first time in eons. "I need to get away from all of this. If it's not the paparazzi then it's my family."

"You should set them all on Joshua. It's his fault anyway. Let him deal with the fallout."

That would be so fantastic. "If only."

"Well. If no one can find you, then they would have no choice, right?"

"And how would I manage that?"

"This is why you made friends with me at boarding school. You never would have survived otherwise."

Anika rolled her eyes. "Just tell me your plan."

"Well, you know who my mum is. I could pull a few strings and get you the hell out of there and into paradise."

It was well known that the famed Claudia Bauer, PA extraordinaire to the equally illustrious James Conroy III, was the gatekeeper to the Totally Five Star world. Anika absolutely believed that Petra could pull some major strings.

"So far this sounds good. What's the catch?"

The melodramatic gasp on the other end of the line made Anika smile.

"Can't a girl help out her friend?"

Anika was well versed in the kind of help Petra was capable of. Some of the time, she came through with flying colors and others were a downright disaster. The number of occasions they'd ended up across the desk getting a dressing down from the head mistress made Anika cringe. The fact that they were usually down to some insane plot hatched by her dear friend didn't instill confidence in Anika.

"So what do you say?" Petra asked eagerly.

What did she have to lose? At the worst, she'd get away from London for a little while. "Okay. Just make sure that it's not going to backfire on me."

Laughter burst on the other end of the line. "When have I ever steered you wrong?"

"The time you got me to sneak out by climbing down the trellis and I fell onto the Head Mistress' car. Or how about when you said no one would ever know it was us who swapped out the soap in the bathroom dispensers with red dye?"

"That was a brilliant one! We never would have gotten caught if it wasn't for the cleaner who told on us."

"Or how about when you thought it would be funny to dump washing powder in the fountain?"

"That was hilarious!"

Anika groaned. "Until it turned into a bubble monster that threatened to devour the grounds."

Petra's laughter tinkled through the phone. "We had some fun, didn't we? And I swear that I'll get you in somewhere great!"

"You'd better or this friendship is over," grumbled Anika. It was a well-worn threat that she never managed to follow through with.

"Bah! You've been saying that for years. You love it and you know it." Petra paused a second before she gasped. "I've got the perfect place! Monaco!"

Anika slapped her hand to her face, nearly mangling her forgotten sunglasses. She righted them and sighed. "I want to lay low."

"It's perfect! You don't have to worry about privacy violations. Have you ever seen paparazzi pics from Monaco?"

Anika racked her already taxed brain. "No."

"That's because paparazzi aren't welcome there. The place might as well be saying 'Come for a visit, Anika De Winter! We're perfect for you!'" Petra barely paused to breathe. "Look, just leave it all to me. Get yourself to Heathrow and I'll take care of the rest."

"Petra…"

"Don't even bother to pack. Just get to the airport. You can thank me later." She clicked off.

Anika banged the phone against her forehead before shoving it back in her bag. She pushed her sunglasses to the top of her head and rubbed her temples. She had to be crazy to let Petra talk her into another one of her schemes.

* * * *

Four hours later, Anika stared in awe at the Totally Five Star Monaco from the back of the limo. The longest part of the trip had been disregarding Petra's advice and trying to figure out what to pack. The rest had been a blur of burgeoning excitement. In spite of the reservations she still had about everything, Anika couldn't help the excitement coursing through her at the thought of leaving the city and getting away from it all.

Monaco was the perfect place to do it, even if she wouldn't admit it to Petra. As her friend had mentioned, there were no paparazzi which made everything that much more enticing. There was plenty to do, and if she didn't want to venture too far, she was sure the hotel would be magnificent and more than worth exploring.

The Totally Five Star Hotels were known for their luxury and exclusive clientele. It was a miracle that Petra was able to get her in. As far as Anika knew, it took connections and a lot of cash to get a reservation. It was good to be friends with daughter of the PA to the owner.

Heart lighter than it had been since before she found herself engaged to Joshua, she almost floated into the magnificent lobby followed by a porter and her few bags. Her heels clicked on the gleaming marble floors as she made her way to the reception desk. She was no stranger to luxurious surroundings, but at the ambiance in the foyer, she slowed her steps so she could get a better look.

The designer had managed to combine a modern and classic look to great effect. The simplicity of the glass geodesic dome above the lobby contrasted with the painted scene around the edge under the arch. The purely decadent style depicted what looked like frolicking mythological beings. Anika took a few steps forward. It was needed to see what had become of them on the other side of the immense glittering chandelier. Curiosity about the fate of the painted characters sated, she took a moment to study the ornate lighting fixture, appreciating the beautiful way it lit the entire room with a warm, glittering glow.

After looking her fill at the ceiling, she let her gaze follow the lines of the dome down one marble pillar. The furnishings in the waiting area looked as inviting as they did expensive. The polished wood of the legs and frames cradled the plush, subtly patterned creamy fabric. Anika let her observation follow the carefully arranged settees, chairs and tables. The scent of the fresh flowers weighed the air, drifting in delicate wafts in the unseen breeze. The ambiance immediately made her feel welcome, relaxed.

Study done, Anika inhaled the scent again as she made her way toward the desk and the immaculately dressed woman patiently waiting there. Her midnight black hair pinned up in a classic chignon at the back of her neck. Her crisp white blouse cut a blinding line against the perfect black of her skirt. Her striking red lips parted in a brilliant smile that lit up the room. *Bonne nuit.* Welcome to Totally Five Star Monaco. I'm Marie-Thérèse. How can I be of service this evening?"

Anika smiled in greeting. Even the woman's slightly accented voice brought an air of sophistication. "Anika De Winter, checking in."

"Just one moment." Her French-tipped nails flashed over the keyboard. She paused an instant before furiously typing again.

Anika's stomach hollowed. "Is there a problem?" Of course there was. Petra struck again.

"Just give me another moment, *s'il vous plaît*." She clicked the mouse repeatedly and typed briskly for another few seconds.

"It's fine. Really." She motioned for the porter to take the bags back outside. "Please call for another limo."

"No, no, Ms. De Winter. It has all been sorted. I just missed a memo, but everything is in order." She slipped a key card across the counter.

Anika picked it up, but still wasn't entirely convinced. "Thank you. If you'll give me a moment."

"But of course." Marie-Thérèse nodded, though she looked a little reticent. "I hope I haven't upset you."

"Not at all." Anika pulled out her phone and dialed Petra.

She picked up after three rings. "Hey, babes, you get there okay?"

"I just checked in."

"Fabulous!"

Anika sighed. "Not really, the woman had a hard time finding me on the system. Any idea why?"

"Did she?"

Anika wasn't fooled by the innocent tone in her friend's voice. "What's going on?"

"It's no big deal. I just had another guest moved so that you could get in."

She rubbed her temple. "What do you mean moved?" Anika turned away from the desk and snarled "You bumped someone for me?" The outraged gasp that came from the other end of the line made her pinch the bridge of her nose.

"That sounds so horrible! I made sure she was compensated. Relax."

How could Anika relax? "I can't believe you did that!"

"I did it for you." Petra sighed. "It's too late now. She's out. You're in. End of story."

"You're unbelievable."

"Just take the suite. Get some sleep. You'll feel better in the morning. If anything goes wrong — and nothing will — it will come back on me. Not you."

The weight that had finally started to lift fell back on Anika like a boulder off a cliff. "I'm too tired to argue. I'll see if I can find another hotel tomorrow."

"Don't be like that. It's all sorted."

"Thanks for all you've done, Petra. I'll call you in a few days." Anika swiped the phone and pressed it to her forehead for a second. She truly was too tired to do anything but crawl into bed, curl up in a ball and sleep.

"Is everything okay, Ms. De Winter?" Marie-Thérèse watched on with concern etched on her face.

"Wonderful. Which way to my room?"

"Marcel will show you the way. You will find everything you require in your suite. If there is anything I can do to make your stay even more pleasant, don't hesitate to ring down. Please enjoy your stay."

Anika made her best attempt at a smile, but it felt lackluster, even to her. "I'm sure I will."

* * * *

The porter swept open the door to her suite and stepped aside. Anika shuffled in feeling like an interloper in someone else's home. How could Petra do this to her? Why did she let her friend talk her into these stupid plots of hers? Again. It was just another on a long line of mistakes that she let herself be dragged into.

She reached into her purse to find a tip, just wanting him to be gone so she could wallow in yet another bad life choice. He said something about enjoying her stay, she handed him the handsome gratuity, then he disappeared down the hall.

Anika kicked the door closed and surveyed the suite. The living area was well decorated. Like the rest of the hotel, it was a blend of modern and florid classical designs and there was a lightness to the color scheme. The fabrics were all creamy white with a subtle pattern to add interest. She ran her fingers over the pale, polished wood of the little table near the door. Vases bursting with flowers sat on polished tables of matching wood throughout the room.

She kicked off her shoes to scrunch her toes into the plush carpet as she wandered. Anika followed the edge of a large rug as she took in the well-chosen art decorating the walls. That artist was unknown to her — perhaps a new talent — but she admired the bold strokes even when the color choice was soothing and restful. She delicately ran her fingers over the painting on the wall as she passed. No, definitely not a print.

Anika liked the mix of modern and classic styles. If it were all modern, it would have been too austere while the other way around would have been an overwhelming assault on her senses.

She flowed from room to room admiring the restraint that had gone into the design and decoration of the suite, her favorite rooms being the gloriously decadent bedroom and bathroom. Anika knew if she wasn't going to be in the massive bed watching the boats in the harbor through the floor-to-ceiling windows, she would be lounging in the almost equally huge bath testing the contents of the various bottles provided by the hotel.

By the time she had done a full circle, her nerves had calmed somewhat and Anika started to regret how she'd spoken to Petra. Her friend was only trying to help her out—in her own, strange way.

But first, she would get some room service. Anika picked up the menu and browsed it as she dialed. Minutes later, she had ordered a small three-course meal, baked scallops in licorice-flavored crust to start, an entrée of bouillabaisse, with a dark chocolate soufflé for dessert, accompanied by a bottle of Bollinger.

Order made, Anika crossed the room to open the French doors that led onto the balcony. The fresh sea air beckoned her over to the stand at the railing to admire the view while she waited. Watching the yachts in the harbor against the backdrop of a magnificent sunset calmed her further. Maybe this had been a good idea after all?

A muted ping from her phone made her look over her shoulder but she couldn't muster the energy or the interest to go searching for it. Her mother hadn't stopped hounding her with calls and texts since Anika had left one telling her parents she was going away for a while. Apparently flitting off and hiding wasn't how she was expected to handle the situation. Anika couldn't help blaming them for putting her in the position in the first place.

The last thing she needed was to talk to them and let them bring her down. It was why she hadn't told them where she was going. The last thing she needed was her parents showing up in person and giving her a lecture on the duties of being a De Winter.

All her life she'd been told what to do and who to do it with. Every inch of her life had been delineated with rules. As she'd gotten older, she found they only grew in number and got tighter in constraint.

Sighing, she leaned over the wrought-iron balustrade to look down at the shimmering indigo water. She'd figure things out. But she had to do it on her own without anyone else whispering in her ear.

What she wanted to do now was just be herself, enjoy her time away, and just shut everything else out.

The abrupt knock at the door drew her attention. Anticipating room service, Anika hurried to the door. She was more than ready for food and a good champagne to wash it down. The fact that more than two glasses of champagne would incapacitate her didn't hurt either. Maybe numbness would be just what the doctor ordered.

Anika opened the door with a practiced smile on her face but rather than be greeted by a waiter with a cart of food, there was a darkly handsome man in an exquisite suit, the expectant smile on his face waning when his gaze alighted on her.

"Where's Danielle?"

His voice was like warmed honey, the slight accent she caught telling her he was Italian, as did his dark eyes and hair. The powerfully built man towered over her by at least a head, while his broad shoulders filled her vision and his long legs added to an already alluring package that made her wonder what was under the impeccably tailored black suit and crisp white shirt. She followed the long, lean line of his body down to his shoes before traveling back upward. When she got to his face again, Anika realized that he was familiar, not someone she knew personally, but she'd seen him before.

As she made her appraisal, he did the same to her. The scowl on his face morphed into blatant male interest as his gaze swept over her. He smiled and extended his hand. "Luca Rossi."

And just like that, all interest in him died, as if he'd thrown a bucket of ice water over her.

Anika stumbled backward and slammed the door in his face.

Chapter Two

Luca stared at the closed door, stunned but mildly amused. Well, that was new. The striking raven-haired beauty reacted as if he'd assaulted her. He was only responding to the look she'd given him. He knew when a woman wanted him — and she had. So what had just happened?

He'd only introduced himself.

He stared at the door a moment longer and was about to leave when a waiter trundled up the hall pushing a cart. From the way the man was looking at him, Luca knew where he was trying to go.

Luca smiled at the young man. "Thank you. I'll take it in."

The waiter didn't look so sure. "I should do it myself."

"Not at all, you've brought it to the door. I can take it in myself." Luca slipped a very generous tip into his hand. "No one will ever know."

Nodding, the waiter stepped back. "As you wish. Enjoy the meal, *monsieur*."

"I will." Luca waited patiently for the man to disappear down the hall before knocking on the door again.

This time her voice came through the door. "Who is it?"

"Room service."

The door opened again. He watched as her smile wilted.

"What do you want?"

"To bring in your room service." He indicated to the cart as he pushed it into the room.

"Thank you." She glared at him witheringly as she held the door open, clearly waiting for him to leave.

Luca didn't take the hint. "So what was that?"

"What?"

"Don't play innocent. One second you were undressing me with your eyes, but the moment I tell you my name, you slam the door in my face."

"I was not!" Forgotten, the door fell closed behind her as she pressed her hands to her cheeks to hide the flush there. "Please leave right now before I'm forced to call security."

"Not until you tell me why." Luca stepped closer and crossed his arms, pleased when her cheeks grew even rosier. She might not want to admit it, but she *was* affected by his presence.

"You dated a friend of mine."

He arched an eyebrow. "Did I? Would this friend have a name?"

"Honoria Blackwood."

Luca nodded. He remembered Honoria well. "And I take it her review of me was less than glowing."

"It most definitely was." Her eyes flashed angrily at him. "You treated her abysmally!"

He took it all in, sighing when she glared at him. "Are you done?"

"Yes."

Luca crowded her and she took a half step back.

"Did it ever occur to you that she made that all up?"

She crossed her arms over her chest protectively. "Why would she do that?"

"To save face? Could it not be possible that your dear friend was the one who cheated on me? And not only that but she was so unbelievably cavalier about it that she was caught out?"

The woman before him paled a little. Her brilliant sapphire eyes wide as she stared up at him. "You're a liar."

"Why is it so easy to believe her over me? Were you there? You don't know me. From the sound of it, you barely know her."

Anika balked. "I never said she was a dear friend."

He kept his gaze leveled on hers. He was right. It was a knee-jerk reaction at information that might not have been from the best source.

Anika had run into Honoria at a fundraiser the year before where she'd told Anika the story. It had seemed odd to her, after not seeing her in such a long time, that Honoria would share such a personal account. But she'd heard similar stories so many times before that she'd simply accepted it without analysis. And why shouldn't she? Up until now, she had never met the man. His reputation was more than enough to color her judgment of him.

She knew more than anyone did how wrong a reputation could be.

Anika pursed her lips as she capitulated. "I'm sorry. It was wrong of me to judge you."

"Thank you." He smiled magnanimously. "So what are we eating?" Luca lifted the silver dome off one of the trays and inhaled.

For a man who was just harping on about manners, he had some strange ideas about dining with strangers. "*I've* only ordered a small meal." She watched as he nodded and pulled the Bollinger out of the ice bucket. He nodded again when he looked at the label.

"I'm sure you wouldn't mind sharing your champagne. All this for one as petite as yourself? I think not."

She tried to take it from him but he held it out of reach. Unwilling to back down, she glared at him. "You don't know me. I could be a raging alcoholic who drinks three of those a day."

"You're right. I don't because you slammed the door in my face instead of introducing yourself when I tried the last time." His smile was challenging when he looked at her. "Shall we try this again?" He held out his hand. "Luca Rossi."

Anika took it. The instant his hand engulfed hers, she felt a frisson of electricity pinball through her. It flared again when his gaze collided with hers. "Anika De Winter."

"A pleasure."

The way he practically purred the word sent shivers skittering through her. She looked at the door. "So…"

"So now we've been properly introduced, having dinner together isn't so strange, is it?" He sat on one of the pristine white sofas. "I'll just order another portion for myself."

Anika couldn't believe his gall. "You weren't invited to join me."

"A beautiful woman shouldn't eat alone." He picked up the phone and started dialing. "Especially not isolated in a room, even one as lovely as this. So I'm going to remedy one offense."

Crossing her arms, she glared at him. "So this is for *my* benefit?"

"Of course." The easy smile almost made her believe it. Almost.

"Do you just do whatever you like whenever you like?"

"Usually." He put the phone down. "I'm sensing displeasure."

"You're incredibly astute." Anika motioned to the door again. "I'm sure I'll be seeing you around during my stay."

Luca didn't stand. He leaned forward, elbows on his knees, his fingers laced together. "Speaking of your stay…"

Her stomach dropped. "Wh—what about it?"

"I know for a fact Danielle da Costa was booked into this room for this weekend."

She gritted her teeth. "How can you be so sure?"

"Because I made the reservation for this room specifically." Point made, he coolly leaned back in his chair like a king passing judgment on a peasant. "So I'm assuming you managed to bribe your way in without a care for the damage you've done to others' plans."

She wasn't going to reveal Petra's part in this to him. Anika shook her head. "Maybe that's how you do things, but I managed to get this room by pure luck. Perhaps your lady friend changed her mind."

"I'll soon find out." He reached for the phone again. "So should I be calling down to reception to find out what went wrong or should I call for room service?"

What could she do? What it basically came down to was when would she rather be kicked out—now or later? Sighing, she waved at the phone. "Order your meal." She wanted at least to eat first before she had to find another hotel.

"Thank you."

He called and ordered a feast. Apparently, he didn't think she'd ordered enough for herself—either that or he had a huge appetite. Her thoughts drifted to his body. If he ate as much as that, he would have to work out all day long to keep his physique.

Anika mentally shook off the thought. Who cared? The man was a temporary thorn in her side. The moment the meal was over, she would move hotels and she'd never see him again. The thought buoyed her heart a little.

"You have a lovely smile." Luca put the phone down and studied her openly. Closely.

His voice was enough to extinguish the little spark of hope and the way he observed her made her stomach flutter.

"You don't like me, do you?" he asked.

"Why should I? So far, I know nothing about you but secondhand information from a woman who apparently hates you, then you invite yourself into my room and blackmail me into having dinner with you. What's there to like?" Anika started pacing. "All I wanted was time alone. Away from…everything. And nothing has gone as it was supposed to. Nothing! I was an idiot for thinking I could trust—" She released a slow breath and cursed. "Serves me right for trusting anyone. Enjoy your meal."

Anika stomped over to her bags, yanked the pull handles out then dragged them to the door.

He watched in mild horror as the cool beauty before him unraveled within seconds. He'd teased but hadn't meant to push her beyond her limits. He hadn't guess just how close she was to the edge.

Luca stepped in her path. He wasn't a cruel person. Hurting others didn't appeal to him — unless they had done something to warrant it.

Anika De Winter, however, did not. He didn't make a habit of pushing his presence on women. Nor did he usually find himself so intrigued with a woman he had only just met. Sure, he'd experienced lust at first sight, but fascination? That was something new. He wasn't ready for her to walk out of his life just yet.

"Calm down. I was only teasing. If it's that important that you have your solitude, you can have it. I just thought you could enjoy the company." He put up his hands. "Look we're both here alone tonight. I could do with someone to share what is sure to be a spectacular meal. You've obviously only just arrived. You need a rest. You'll feel better afterward. Make a decision then."

Her vivid blue eyes followed his hand when he motioned to the couch. She was exhausted. He could see it in her face, her rounded shoulders and unsteady gait. But it was more than just jet lag. He felt the inexplicable urge to wipe away the fatigue and replace it with a smile.

Luca didn't let her take another step toward the door. Instead, he pressed a gentle hand to the small of her back and guided her to the couch. And just in time. The moment she settled on the couch there was a knock at the door. He quickly moved the suitcases into the closet, shut them behind the door and swept open the other. The same waiter stood proud and straight with another, bigger cart. This one nearly overflowed with domes on both levels. "Room service."

"Thank you." As before, he took control of the cart after giving the waiter yet another fat wad of bills.

"Thank you, *monsieur*. Have a pleasant evening." The waiter gave him a big grin and a slight bow before hurrying back down the hall.

With all the money he'd given him between this meeting and their last, it was amazing he wasn't skipping. Luca shut the door, then wheeled the cart in to stop in front of the coffee table. "Why don't we take this on the verandah? It's a beautiful evening."

Anika shrugged. "Sure, why not?"

Undeterred by her apathy, he walked out and set the food on the table. He helped her into her seat then filled their glasses one at a time with the sparkling gold liquid. "The fresh sea air always invigorates me."

The look she gave him could be called withering at best. But she at least looked at the food with some interest. Luca took a bit off every tray and placed it on her plate before doing the same to his.

He glanced at her while she ate. Her pale skin gained some color, but it was obvious that she was never tan to begin with. Luca recognized her name and knew a little about her family. The De Winters were well known for their gems. It seemed their heiress truly was as cool and icy as one of their famed diamonds. He'd heard something about her getting married. His scrutiny dropped to her left hand. Or not. Was that why she was so sullen? A broken engagement? He couldn't blame her if it was. But what kind of moron would jilt such a beauty? And one so wealthy at that? He could only guess that the man was a complete fool.

Luca didn't bother wasting any more thought on the other man. He had better things to do with his time. The thought occurred that they could both use a little R & R. He had booked this little break with Danielle, a woman of his acquaintance that was as happy as he was to continue with their casual dalliances. She was beautiful, sophisticated, and found the idea of pairing off totally abhorrent just as he did. Though, to be honest, she was beginning to bore him and he'd only invited her along because he knew she was free.

Danielle getting bumped for Anika couldn't have been better. The challenge of getting to know the De Winter heiress was appealing as a diversion. Seeing if he could break the frosty shell would be worth the work. He could imagine her passionate as she was icy once he got her in bed—or over the railing—as the thought started to warm in his mind.

He shifted in his seat as his cock hardened at the thought of Anika crying out beneath him as she crested.

It could be a very fun weekend, indeed.

As Anika ate—and the fatigue clouding her mind cleared a little—she realized that she was being observed. Thoroughly.

It was unnerving being watched like prey. Or was it being hunted by a man like Luca Rossi that upset her equilibrium?

Luca was handsome, without a doubt. But she'd dealt with her fair share of handsome men. The ones who knew they were attractive swaggered around as if they were in possession of a precious commodity. The ones who didn't at first, turned into complete asses once they figured it out. She'd also met with more than her share of millionaires, billionaires and other tycoons with more zeroes in their bank accounts than brain cells. They all seemed to think money made up for deficits in their personalities. If her experience was anything to go by, Luca Rossi should have been arrogant, brainless and have as much character as a sack of rocks.

So why wasn't she in a limo traveling away from him as fast as possible?

Because she was tired. That was all. Not because he'd blackmailed her into it, not that she found his take-charge nature and the quick gear-shift into considerate an interesting dichotomy. And most definitely not because he was so attractive it made her want to sit and stare at him. Or oddly charming, in an overbearing kind of way. She was just overwrought from everything that had been going on and she needed a moment to recharge.

She speared the scallop and sliced into it as if she was going for its heart. It was the last one on her plate. Anika made a point of eating only what she had ordered. Only she hadn't realized how hungry she was and the rest looked and smelled mouth-watering.

One bite wouldn't hurt.

Anika knew what each dish was after reading the menu and took a forkful of the delicate looking sea bream. It melted on her tongue. Sighing with delight, she swallowed and tried a little of the duckling. It earned another gratified moan. Anika looked at her companion when she saw him tense. "Something wrong?"

"Not at all." His words might have sounded flippant, but his voice sounded choked.

Anika watched him a moment longer before returning her attention to the delicious meal. "The meal is fantastic. The chef here is a magician."

Her attempt at small talk fell on deaf ears. He was the one who had forced his presence on her and now he wasn't talking? The man was an enigma. There was more than enough to keep her senses occupied. The food, the view, the air—he had been absolutely right about the air—and the food. Now that she was set to rights except for the fatigue, her head was clearer. She had acted abominably toward him. "I apologize for my outburst before. I shouldn't have spoken to you that way."

The mild surprise on his face was quickly masked. "I understand. You've been traveling and are tired. I've been there."

"Thanks for being so understanding."

"I need no thanks." He sighed and sat back with the sparkling glass of champagne. "What I do need is to relax. My guess is you desire the same thing."

Did he know about her woes? It wouldn't surprise her. As far as weddings went, hers was to be the social event of the year. As it turned out it had been, just not for the right reasons. "You would guess correctly."

He took a long, slow sip of his champagne. Anika's attention was drawn to his hand. His long elegant fingers. The strength in them, his jaw. The stubble that had just began to darken it. His beautiful brown eyes were a little dull, weary. Despite the polished veneer, he did seem a bit worn himself.

She waited for him to put the glass down. But before she could say anything, he leveled his unnerving gaze on her.

"Why don't we relax together?"

Anika almost dropped her fork. "If that is a euphemism—"

"I assure you it's not." He sighed. "I'm just saying that we're both here alone."

"I'm not interested in spending time with anyone." Anika pushed her plate away. "Thank you for dinner, but I think it's time you returned to your own room."

He lowered his eyebrows. "Will you hear me out?"

"There's nothing you can say that will change my mind."

"What about you're the reason I'm here alone? I refuse to waste the only vacation I have this year wandering around this place on my own. I think you owe me."

"And if I refuse?"

"Then I'll have to discuss this with my friend, James Conroy III. You might have heard of him. He owns the Totally Five Star Hotels and happens to be a good friend of mine. I'm sure he'll be more than interested that someone in his employ is motivated by a little extra cash than doing a good job."

Her heart was threatening to beat through her ribcage. "It wasn't like that!"

"The result is the same."

Fuming, she glared at him. "You're without entertainment and you want me to do what? Be your geisha for a weekend?"

He rolled his eyes. "Stop being so melodramatic. Just be someone to spend time with. To talk to. You're obviously well to do so you aren't after my money. You've made it more than clear that you have no interest in me physically."

Now she was just a convenience? "So basically I'm no threat to anything you hold dear, which makes it okay to bully your way into my life just to make yours less boring?"

"You make it sound so crass. Let's call it an understanding."

Blood pounded in her ears. He had managed to compel more emotion out of her than anyone else in the past year—and she'd let him. Not only that, she could see he knew it. She might not have liked what Petra did to get her the room, but she didn't want to get her into trouble. Luca Rossi didn't seem to have any compunction in doing anything that got him his way. No doubt, he would point fingers and name names if it got him what he wanted.

She clenched her hands into fists as she got up to pace. "Fine. But I have some rules myself."

A slow smile spread over his sinful lips as he stood as well. "I would be disappointed if you didn't."

She scowled at him. "You won't touch me unless I've given you my express permission."

He held up his hands. "Of course. I am a gentleman, after all."

That was debatable.

"Second. Once the weekend is over, our acquaintance ends."

"So harsh. And what if you change your mind?"

"I won't."

His smiled didn't budge as he stepped in her path just as she would have walked past him. "Very well. Anything else?"

Anika couldn't think with him so close. She could *smell* him. It had to be some sort of cologne. No one's scent could be so enticing. Whatever it was, it made her a little dizzy. "No."

Luca held out his hand sideways. "Then may I seal this deal?"

"You may." She stuck her hand out, expecting him to shake it.

His hand closed around hers and, with a quick jerk, he pulled her against him to capture her mouth with his in a breath-stealing, mind-scrambling kiss.

He tasted heavenly—like champagne and pure man—and he definitely knew how to kiss. Luca expertly parted her lips to gain access, easily plundering her mouth. He delved his tongue deeply and used it to duel with hers. She could taste the dark chocolate of the soufflé mixed with something that was entirely male

Luca dipped her low so he could explore her mouth fully, keeping her off balance leaving her no choice but to cling to him, even though, intuitively, she knew he wouldn't drop her. It was pure instinct when she pressed herself against him. She couldn't stop herself any more than she could stop her nipples from puckering when her breasts grazed his solid chest, or halt the heat blasting through her body.

He plundered. He took. He explored her mouth with stunning expertise. And she wanted more. To feel all of him against her. Taste more of him. From the big, rigid length of him pressed against her, she knew she wasn't the only one affected.

When he finally pulled back, her mind was foggy with just one thought—she wanted more of Luca Rossi.

The smug smile he gave her wiped the thought away and she slammed her hands into his shoulders. He didn't budge.

"How dare you!"

"I asked for permission and you gave it to me. It wasn't my fault you didn't ask for specifics."

The grin he gave her was wide and wolfish when she huffed at him.

"Thank you for a lovely evening. I'll see you in the morning."

Anika fought the childish urge to stick her tongue out at him when he winked and walked out of the door as if nothing had transpired.

She picked up the sweating glass of ice-cold champagne and held it to her cheek while she tried to rein in whatever it was rampaging through her body.

What the hell had just happened?

The thought chased through her mind the rest of the night.

Chapter Three

Anika stared out over the water, her second — or was it her third? — espresso in hand, as she watched the sun creep over the horizon. Just like the sunset the night before, it was awe-inspiring. The bands of pink slowly warmed into orange and gold until fingers of sunlight stretched up and turned the sky the blazing blue that captivated her. How did anyone who lived here get anything done? She would probably waste the daylight hours staring out at the harbor and the nights gazing up at the mesmerizing sparkle of the stars. What was it about this place that made even the most mundane thing seem extraordinary?

Over her restless night, she had come to the conclusion that Monaco wove a spell on her that made her think that everything was more magical — including a kiss from a man she didn't know. She'd even spent part of the night searching the Internet for information to prove herself right about him. The only thing she had to go on was business sites that touted him as the best thing to ever venture into capitalism and trashy scandal sheets that had him painted as a rake and scandalous playboy.

Anika knew just how much faith to put into those reports. They were on the same pages that showed her 'traumatized' from Joshua's abandonment. He seemed to be another favorite topic for Pink Poison. The very same blogger that loved to hound Anika. And she knew just how much 'research' that woman did for her stories. She had put the phone down not knowing if she was more disgusted by the life he was supposed to lead or the woman who penned all the awful stories.

Her phone pinged and vibrated, almost sending itself off the balustrade where she had traded it for the espresso after the last Internet search frenzy. She caught it with nimble fingers just as it tilted off the edge, though she was tempted to let it fall so she could watch it shatter. Only Anika couldn't be that irresponsible. A quick check revealed another handful of texts and several emails crammed into her rapidly filling inboxes. She ignored the ones from her family, briskly answered work ones then dropped the device onto the sun lounger.

She would deal with family later. Her father had been grooming her to take over the De Winter Group. Nothing he had been 'teaching' her over the past few years was anything she hadn't already learned by observing him as a child. Business school had filled in the gaps and she was confident that assuming control would be straightforward enough. She was already heading up certain aspects of the business, preferring to handle the PR side of things than the day-to-day monotony. Her father still delighted in reminding her that she would have to deal with everything else once she was ready.

The nebulous threat of one day was fine with her. Roland De Winter was still young and robust enough to control that side of things for many years to come. By then, she hoped he would find someone else more interested in numbers and bean counting to manage the company.

Joshua would have been good in that capacity. It was probably one of the reasons her father had pushed for the marriage in the first place. But after her successful ad campaigns over the past couple of years, their stocks were on the rise again. A point that her father didn't seem to notice when he and Joshua's father put their heads together and came up with the genius idea of joining their families with a big, showy wedding and a marriage of convenience. At least, it was convenient for them. She and Joshua had been blindsided, hogtied with familial loyalty and dragged to the altar.

Sighing, she finished off the espresso and wished she had another. The little sleep she had managed to get had been plagued with images of Luca. For some reason, her subconscious seemed to prefer him naked and doing wicked things to her that left her aching when she woke. She'd finally given up some time before dawn preferring to look up salacious reports of him than imagining her own scenarios.

Those had proven to be too tempting and devastating for a good night's sleep.

Which left her even more fatigued, grumpy and definitely not looking forward to spending any time with the man who had inspired the dreams. Where did he get off blackmailing her into spending time with him? Who did he think he was?

One thing was for sure — no more falling for any more of Petra's so-called 'genius' schemes.

She wandered through the suite and headed for the bathroom. What she needed was a good, long soak to relax her. Anika laughed ruefully as she turned on the gleaming taps with a twist. She'd need another vacation to recover from this one.

Anika had barely managed to warm up from the water before there was knocking at the door. There would be only one person who would dare at this hour.

She grabbed the robe on her way out and wrapped it securely around herself. Taking a fortifying breath, she opened the door to find Luca on the other side as she'd expected. "It's a bit early, isn't it?"

"You're up, aren't you?" His grin contrasted handsomely with his tan skin. "May I?"

"I guess I ought to or you'll go running to your friend to tattle on me."

He laughed as he walked past.

Allured by the timbre of his laugh, Anika watched him walk through as if he owned the place. She caught the whiff of his cologne and had to stop herself from following him to catch more. What the hell was wrong with her? Biting her bottom lip, she closed the door. He stood at the balcony surveying the scene like a king perusing his kingdom. Luca was handsome. The suit was gone, replaced with jeans and a pristine white button-down shirt left untucked and unbuttoned at the top, giving her a tantalizing glimpse of tan skin. The man made casual wear look good. Someone so infuriating had no right appearing so enticing.

"I thought we could explore the harbor before it got too hot."

Stretching her legs did have appeal. "Sounds lovely. Have you had breakfast yet?"

He shook his head as he noted the array of cups on the coffee table. "Restless night?"

"Threats to be kicked out of a hotel at any moment aren't exactly lullabies."

He frowned but said nothing as he picked up the phone and dialed room service. "I'd like breakfast for two brought up." He brusquely made a few alterations to the menu, gave the room number and hung up.

Anika waved at herself. "If it's all right with you, I'd like to get dressed." Goodness knew what the staff thought of constantly seeing him in her suite ordering room service as if he belonged there. The last thing she needed was perpetuating any rumors by being caught in a robe by the waiter. She was already on her way to the bedroom when she heard his lazy reply.

"By all means."

She closed the door securely behind her, hating that he had her so off kilter. Instead of letting the realization get to her, she focused her efforts on getting dressed.

Her barb about his threat to have her kicked out had hit a nerve. But what did he expect? The truth of the matter was that he *had* blackmailed her into spending time with him. No one would accept that gracefully. His goal now was to smooth the feathers he'd ruffled — and what feathers they were.

After the kiss they had shared the night before, he had no hope of falling asleep. Instead, he expended the pent-up energy in the hotel pool. Even after several dozen laps, his body refused to relax, needing more sensual stimulation that he refused to look for elsewhere. So he spent the early hours of the morning learning as much as he could about Anika De Winter.

Luckily for him, her whole life was at his fingertips.

She was only a handful of years younger than him, though she looked much younger. The sole heiress to the CEO of the De Winter Group, she had enjoyed a life of privilege and had gone to boarding school in Switzerland, business school in London and was now managing PR for the DWG. And she was doing very well with it, if the stocks analysts were telling the truth. Their fortunes had taken an upswing since she'd come on the scene.

The Ice Princess was well known for her cool exterior and lack of interest in anything other than her job. It came as a shock to many when she and her fiancé had announced their engagement less than a year ago. A whirlwind romance it was called. Luca knew a marriage of convenience when he saw one.

He considered her lucky for escaping what was sure to be a miserable fate. He knew of plenty of men who had entered into such deals thinking that it would be easy only to end up mired in wretchedness.

As far as he was concerned, they had put themselves in the situation so when they moaned to him about it, he had no sympathy whatsoever.

He deliberately steered his mind away from his glum musings. What he wanted to do now was show her that there was more to life than work and familial obligations. To see if he could crack the Ice Princess' diamond-hard veneer.

She emerged from the room just as breakfast arrived, surprisingly. He had been resigned on waiting the rest of the morning for her to get ready, but was pleasantly proven wrong. Not only was she quick at dressing but she wore attire so simple he was charmed. Gray, wide-legged pants and a simple white silk tank top with thin straps. Even her makeup, what traces he could see, was light. Not that she needed it. Her dark hair and fair skin gave her a dramatic look that didn't need augmentation. Her lashes were full and surrounded her feline-like eyes enhancing them to spectacular effect. He dropped his gaze to the lips he had tasted the night before, which were pink and full, beckoning him to sample them again…

His body responded to his wayward thoughts.

Luca waved at the newly arrived cart. "Help yourself."

"Mind if we eat on the verandah again?" She brushed a lock of hair over the pale curve of her shoulder.

"Not at all." He pushed the cart to the doors, helped her into her seat then placed the trays on the table.

"I could get used to this." Anika smirked at him as he lifted the domes. "We've had two meals together and you've served me both times."

Luca found he didn't mind, neither the part where he presented her with food nor her ribbing. It made a change from her sniping at him. It was a good sign. "Perhaps we should do something other than the harbor today? The sun's already hot and I fear you would burn to a crisp."

She looked at the scenery and nodded. "What else did you have in mind?"

"Have you ever been here before?" He sipped his coffee, watching her over the rim.

"I have." Her cheeks turned a light pink. "But I must confess that I haven't gone farther than conference rooms and meeting halls."

"You don't know what you're missing." A myriad of ideas flashed through his mind before he snapped his fingers, certain he'd figured out the best thing to do. "If you give me a few minutes to make the arrangements, I've got a brilliant activity for us to enjoy this morning."

Anika delicately sipped her tea. "Care to share?"

"I think I'll leave it a surprise." He arched an eyebrow at her. "If you think you can handle it, that is."

Anika knew he was baiting her. She wasn't going to let him get to her. However, there was no way she was going to back down from a direct challenge. "I can handle anything."

The smile he gave her was a dare—pure and simple. "Good."

Chapter Four

Anika held onto the handle with a white-knuckled grip, but was exhilarated more than she was scared. It wasn't the first time she'd been in a helicopter, though the things still scared the wits out of her. This time, however, was as thrilling as it was terrifying. For some reason, she attributed it to the man next to her. He was the self-appointed tour guide for the trip and made her forget her fear, for the most part.

His sharp comments and the distraction of the gorgeous scenery, not to mention the warmth of his hand curled around hers when the flight got a little choppy, kept all her senses too occupied to worry.

Luca was quite knowledgeable about the area, and the pilot threw in some facts that he didn't know as well, as they swooped over the tiny principality. Anika hadn't realized so much time could be spent exploring the tiny patch of land from the air. But thirty minutes later, she still wanted more.

Luca got out first and took her hand to help her down. "So?"

It had been amazing, but Anika played it down not wanting him to get too big headed for making their first outing a resounding success. "It was nice."

"It was." He sounded a little surprised.

Anika pulled her hand gently from his grasp. "What shall we do now? Head back to the hotel?"

"There is still so much more to see and do." He cocked his head to look at her. "Unless you've had enough for one day."

She checked her watch, not wanting to look too eager. "It's still early, I guess."

"There are museums we could check out."

She cocked her head. "You can do better than that, surely."

A wolfish grin spread slowly over his lips, until they parted, giving her a glimpse of perfect teeth. "Are you up for another adrenaline rush?"

Absolutely. She nodded slightly. "I suppose."

He took her hand and pulled her toward the waiting limo. Luca helped her in but didn't follow. Anika could hear him speaking with someone, arranging something. It took her a moment to realize he spoke with someone at the hotel who could pull strings. From the sound of it, they had some major clout. Not surprising for a hotel of Totally Five Star's caliber, even if what he asked for sounded like an impossibility. It took seconds more for him to realize she was listening and closed the door with a knowing smile. Not a minute later, he opened the door and slid into the seat next to her.

Luca dominated the small space with his presence. It wasn't just because his wide shoulders filled most of the seat. It was *him*. Anika fought not to slide aside. She wasn't going to allow him to crowd her into a corner. Unfortunately, her obstinacy led to a new problem — being too close to Luca.

To move away would show that she was uncomfortable with his proximity. Why should it bother her if she offended him by moving away when he was not much more than a stranger? Yet she couldn't make herself move. And they just kept right on bumping legs.

She couldn't stop her pulse from racing at the touch of his hard thigh against hers. It didn't stop the jolt of electricity that lanced through her whenever they touched. Or when he leveled his gaze on her. It was disconcerting the way he seemed to peer into her soul.

Anika angled her knees slightly so that they were out of the long reach of his.

"Would you like something to drink?"

"I'm fine, thanks." She looked out of the window and watched as the world whipped past. "So where are we headed now?"

"If you'll wait another five minutes, you'll find out." He pulled out a bottled water, and, when she refused it, he deftly unscrewed the cap to take a swig.

She could wait five minutes or she could spend that time needling to see if she could get the information. Since that seemed like more fun, Anika grinned. "I'd rather you told me. I'm not a big fan of surprises."

"You liked the last one."

She pursed her lips. "But I might not like this one. I don't know you. You don't know me. What if your idea of an adrenaline rush puts me to sleep?"

"It won't."

"You're awfully sure of yourself."

"So I'm self-assured. I'm told that's a good thing."

Anika shrugged at him. "It can be. Until it crosses the line to arrogance."

He put the bottle down and smirked at her. "Are you calling me arrogant?"

"Well, let's see. Since we've met, you've been nothing but arrogant, so I think I reserve the right to call you that."

"According to whose definition? I know what I want and how to get it. Just because they don't coincide with behavior you deem humble doesn't make me arrogant."

She grinned at him. "And that was a pretty arrogant thing to say."

He smirked. "Then, I guess by your standards, I'm an arrogant man."

"Very much so. You can prove me wrong by at least giving me a little detail to where we are headed."

Chuckling, he leaned back and regarded her steadily. "Let me get this straight. I can prove I'm not arrogant by giving into your equally haughty attempt at coercion?"

"I didn't make any demands. I was just having a conversation." Anika chuckled. She knew he was playing with her. Just as he knew she was needling him. She enjoyed it—the back and forth. Not having to worry if he got her or not. He did. Or at least he seemed to. He could just be very good at reading people or knew how to give women what they wanted in general. It would make sense if he were as good with the ladies as the media would have people believe. Or it could have to do with his money or his skills in bed...

The less she thought about that, the better. Anika shifted in her seat. What she felt was attraction to him. She wasn't an idiot. Dating might not have been her thing, but she knew chemistry when she felt it. It was just preferable to ignore it. Shove it aside. Relationships were messy. Complicated things. It was best avoided. She knew people called her Ice Princess behind her back. She didn't know what bothered her more about the name—the lack of creativity or the image that it purveyed. But after some creative marketing, Anika used the name to her benefit, making it synonymous with Diamond Princess. Which became the keystone of her ad campaign. Now every woman in the world wanted to be a De Winter Ice Princess.

"We're here."

Luca's voice drew her attention first to him then to the scene out of the window on his side of the car. It looked like they were parked on the edge of the road overlooking a cliff overlooking the ocean. Interest piqued, she leaned over to get a better look. "I'll admit, I have no idea what you have in mind."

He waggled his brows at her and stepped out into the bright sunshine.

Anika took his hand and let him help her out. The bracing sea air whipped around them as the waves crashed against the base of the cliff. They had to be on one of the Corniche roads. At the front of the limo sat a gleaming silver car. The gull wings were open, reaching into the sky, waiting for them to climb in. So that's what he had planned. A drive along the coast in the gorgeous supercar.

"It's a Pagani Huayra. What do you think?" He stood next to it proudly.

"She's absolutely beautiful." Anika couldn't stop herself from running her fingers over the glossy finish. "Mind if I give her a try?"

Surprise shot his eyebrows upward. "Have you ever driven one of these?"

"No. But I'd love to." She smiled cajolingly.

"I guess you can't do any harm. I'll be right next to you talking you through it." He shrugged. "What can go wrong?"

Anika hid her shock. The car must have cost a small fortune and he was just going to let her drive it? Either Luca had no concept of cost or he actually trusted her. Or perhaps he thought he was such a great a driver that being in the seat next to her would transfer his skill.

She almost laughed aloud at the thought. "So I can?"

He held out his hand. "Whatever you wish. This weekend is about having fun, isn't it?"

"It is." Anika slipped her hands into his with a smile letting him help her in. The supple leather interior cradled her as he relinquished her hand and adjusted the seat and steering column for her.

"How does it feel? Comfortable?" He deftly adjusted the mirrors and talked her through the controls.

Luca knew his way around the vehicle, that much was obvious. And he cared to make sure she was versed enough to run the car competently.

"Ready?" At her nod, he rounded the machine and climbed in. With a smile, he shut the door and turned to her, waiting.

She cautiously pressed the ignition and reveled in the rumbling purr of the engine. Anika eased it onto the road.

Luca watched on as she carefully took the first turn. If he had known she would want to drive, he would have called for a different car and probably picked a road that wasn't carved on the side of a cliff over the ocean.

She eased around the first few curves, getting a feel for the car. It was on the next one that she did something unexpected.

Anika accelerated hard and slung the car around it, pushing it harder and faster with each successive corner. He gripped the door handle the first few times before he realized she knew exactly what she was doing. Once that sank in, he settled back to enjoy the ride as she drifted the car easily, guiding it as if it was an extension of herself.

Luca observed Anika's cool concentration as she pushed the car to its limits. "I thought you said you've never driven one of these before."

"I haven't. It's my first time in a Pagani." She gave him an impish smile. "I've got a Ferrari 458."

He smiled wryly. She had played him. She could handle the machine as well as he could, maybe even better. Luca admired skill. He wondered how many other skills she was hiding. He would wager that beneath the Ice Princess façade smoldered a passionate woman. He could see how her eyes sparkled as she drove. The excitement in them. There was a fire that she kept tightly leashed.

Luca found he wanted to be the one who let it loose. He allowed his mind to volley the different ways he could do it as they sped along the scenic route.

They were almost at Nice when he broke the companionable silence. "How about you give me a turn on the way back? We can take the Moyenne Corniche and get a different perspective and a chance to enjoy it."

She spared him a quick glance. "Not comfortable with a woman driving?"

"Not at all. You're doing admirably. I know men who can't handle a car as well as you do. But you can't enjoy the view as much when you're concentrating on the road. This route needs to be appreciated."

She smiled a little, giving him a curt nod. "Right. We'll switch when we get to Nice."

He smiled. "Why don't we spend some time there? It will give us a chance to stretch our legs."

"I don't see why not."

It looked as though the drive had relaxed her. The stern set of her eyebrows had eased. She even had a slight smile and hadn't immediately shot down his idea to spend time in Nice. Now what to do once they got there? There were a few restaurants he could think of off the top of his head. The beach was always nice. There were clubs but a sunset drive back appealed to him, which would put them off the list. There was plenty to do at night in the area. Luca was sure he could figure out something. And if he couldn't, there would be someone on hand at the hotel who could.

It had to be the first time he'd actually worried so much about entertaining a woman in advance. What was even stranger was that he hardly even knew her. It had to be the challenge. For once, he was faced with a woman who wasn't impressed by his wealth, his position or his job. If anything, *he* was in awe of *her*.

That left a few options — ones that he didn't usually have to resort to. It was alien and strange. But it was uncharted ground and he liked it. She wasn't a simpering female who pretended to be interested in what he liked to get on his good side. The fact that she truly appeared to love cars as he did was a plus. The helicopter ride was fun too. She was clearly afraid in the beginning, but didn't let it stop her. She was entertaining to talk to as well.

Anika De Winter fascinated him.

The realization was met with conflicting emotions — disbelief, amazement and a healthy dose of lust. He wasn't sure how to deal with them all. What he did know was how to handle the lust. And in his experience, once that burned out, they could move on.

A weekend was just the right amount of time to do just that.

Anika basked in the sunlight, stretching as she looked around. Nice was gorgeous and brimming with beautiful, tan people. She stopped at the beachfront alongside several other cars of the same caliber. Lamborghinis, Ferraris, she even spotted a Koenigsegg, among many others. They all looked right at home lined up beachside.

The looks she and Luca received when she stepped out of the driver's side were filled with surprise and even a little derision. Luca handled them with the same aplomb she did.

Anika handed him the keys, their hands grazing as she did. The zap that arced between them made her pause when she would have stepped away. She wasn't sure what came over her, only knowing that she wasn't going to let perfect strangers look down on them. At least that was the excuse she gave herself. "Thanks for letting me drive, darling."

Anika backed him against the car and wound her arms around his neck, dragging his head down to kiss him soundly. She had meant it only to be for show, but the instant her lips touched his, all thoughts blasted from her head.

Luca took full advantage, hooking his hands around her hips and dragging her into him, parting and plundering her mouth with exquisite skill. Anika let herself get swept up in sensations. The hot, wet slide of his tongue against hers distracted her so that she hadn't realized he switched their positions until she was pinned between the car and his solid body.

She tangled her fingers in his hair, anchoring his mouth to hers as he ground his hard erection against the junction of her thighs. Anika's knees wobbled. The searing pleasure was unlike anything she'd ever experienced—wonderful and terrifying all at once.

When she drew back to refill her lungs, she was only dimly aware of the applause coming from the bystanders. All she could focus on was the look in his eyes. She couldn't turn away, mesmerized by their dark depths. If they had been alone, Anika was certain they would be tearing each other's clothes off.

Thank goodness they were on a crowded beach. Not that it stopped her from wanting to rip his shirt off and exploring the muscles she knew were under there.

Luca grinned at her, running his hands through his hair. "You're very welcome."

It took her oxygen-starved mind a second to realize that he was responding to her earlier thanks. She released a slow breath, taking the moment to collect herself. "So what shall we do? It's been a while since I've been here."

He lifted his dark eyebrows. "You actually walked the beach?"

"Once. I can let loose once in a while, you know." Hadn't she just proved that?

Trembling from the aftershocks of his kiss, Anika tamped down the urge to kiss him again. The chemistry between them was too potent. She had to be careful or risk losing her head. And that was something she would never allow to happen.

But what would it be like to kiss him again and open that Pandora's box? She imagined Luca would know what he wanted. And he'd know how to get it. If they had been alone here on the beach, would he have taken her?

She pictured him stripping away her clothes and laying her in the sand. He would explore her body with his hands, his mouth—his tongue. If his popularity with women was true as reported, he would know how to handle her. Luca would know exactly what to do to make her toes curl.

Anika ran the tip of her tongue over her lips as she imagined him doing the same thing much lower down. Heat flared between her thighs and low in her abdomen. The imagined sensation of him kissing and licking her folds was so visceral, she trembled as she looked at him.

Luca watched the emotions flit over her features for an instant before she masked them. He caught uncertainty and fear under the lust. He hadn't needed to study her stunning face to know that she had enjoyed that kiss as much as he had. It had caught him off guard how much he had but he wasn't complaining. She was delectable. The way she responded to him was exactly as he had hoped. Under the icy façade, she was molten. Why did she try so hard to hide it?

She tried hard to hide whatever it was she was thinking from him, but his sharp eyes caught the dilation of her pupils, the speeding up of her breath through her slightly parted lips. Whatever it was Anika imagined, it aroused her greatly. From the way she stared at him, he featured heavily in her fantasy.

What he wouldn't give to see what was going on in her mind.

Did she imagine him taking her right there on the beach? Up against the car? In a corner at a nightclub? He was up for whatever she could come up with.

The thought that Anika had a vivid and dirty imagination sent blood to his already semi-hard cock.

He could see she wasn't ready just yet. But if she had been…

Luca pictured her naked on the sand, burnished by the light of the setting sun, begging him to take her. Pleading with him as he plunged into her tight, wet slit. It would feel incredible.

His gaze collided with hers and, for an instant, Luca was sure she would utter the words that would break his control.

Instead, Anika broke eye contact and looked up and down the beach, the slight breeze wafting her scent over him. His groin tightened even more. He needed to sink into her, bring them both immeasurable pleasure, until they were both trembling and replete. Just not right now. "I know of a place where we can get something to eat before we head back."

"That's great. Is it close?"

"It's not too far." He toed off his shoes and bent to take off his socks.

"Do we have to wade into the ocean to get there?"

"No, but walking along the waterline is preferable to the crowded sidewalk." He tossed the discarded items of clothing into the car and looked pointedly down at her feet, clearly expecting her to do the same with her shoes.

Anika relented. Taking off her shoes, she retrieved them then hung them from his waiting fingers.

He tossed them in without a second thought and held out his hand. "Shall we?"

She'd pretty much accosted him in public. What could it hurt to do something as benign as take his hand?

Anika placed her hand in his and it fit into his neatly. When he interlocked their fingers, she looked at him, ducking away before his gaze could meet hers. It felt nice. Comfortable. However, the tingle that shot up her arm at his touch felt like so much more.

He led them toward the water. A slow amble as if they had all the time in the world. Anika inhaled the salted sea air, loving the sensation of not having a timetable to stick to. No deadlines. No one asking questions. Nothing to prepare. She could just relax.

Only she couldn't. Not when she was so near Luca. She was edgy — twitchy — and she didn't like it. Perhaps it was because she was so close to such a virile man. But she'd been stuck in boardrooms for hours with men. Ones just as potent as Luca, or so their swagger would have anyone in the vicinity believe. She never felt a thing. Yet here, with Luca, she couldn't stop staring at his handsome face. And whenever he looked at her, she felt every glance as if he'd reached out and touched her. Anika wanted to know why.

The kisses that they had shared had been good — more than good. It was something she wanted to do again. Time spent with Luca could be just what she needed. If her reaction to him was anything to go by, he could be the diversion she needed.

She had always done her best to follow the rules, play it safe. It had gotten her a successful career, but what else?

What she wanted to do right now was play with fire—with Luca.

Her phone pinged as if to remind her that she still had a job to do. Like she could forget.

His gaze drifted to her phone. "Do you need to get that?"

"I don't need to. I should, but I'm not going to."

Luca's smile was little more than a quirk of his lips. "You sound like a petulant child rebelling."

She chuckled. "Maybe I am." Anika concentrated on the feeling of the sand beneath her feet. The warmth crept up her legs as they walked. The surging waves brought with them a fragrant breeze. The combination of it all helped her muscles slowly un-bunch. She let herself imagine what it would be like to be here with a loved one. That she was simply enjoying time with a man who mattered to her.

Not that she had anything to go on besides the romance novels she'd read as a teen, dreaming about what true love would be like. That the man for her would be smart, sexy, romantic, handsome and overall drool worthy. No man had ever met her expectations. The ones whom she had given a chance had let her down terribly. Maybe it was time to forget about expectations? To just let loose and have fun?

That kiss she'd given him earlier had been a huge leap for Anika. She hadn't thought it through. Didn't weigh the pros and cons. She'd done it on a whim and it had been fun—pleasurable—and the earth hadn't opened up and swallowed her whole for not following a plan.

Her thoughts were derailed when Luca spun her around and pulled her into his arms. "You're thinking too hard. We're on vacation."

The way he said *we're* made something behind her belly button flutter. "The irony? I was thinking about not thinking."

Luca chuckled as he unwound her from his grasp. He kept hold of her hand as they continued down the beach. "I suppose we both have the tendency to overthink things."

Something else they had in common.

"So where are we going?"

"I found a little place in the old town a few years ago. Whenever I'm here, I visit it."

"Must be good." Anika imagined the restaurant glittered with Michelin stars.

"It is." He led them up to the sidewalk.

Anika balked. "I don't have my shoes." She arched a brow at him accusingly. Did he have enough money to make people look the other way for walking into a restaurant of that caliber without shoes?

"Not a problem." Luca hunkered in front of her. "Get on."

"You're kidding."

"I'm not." He looked at her over his shoulder. "It's either this or I carry you over my shoulder. Or maybe I'll just cradle you like a baby. Your choice."

"Charming." Anika couldn't imagine a worse way of being carried than with her ass in the air, so she chose to climb onto his back, clinging to him for dear life. He stood easily and adjusted his grip as he walked.

Knowing he couldn't see her, she smiled. Truly grinned. She couldn't think of another time she'd ridden piggyback. Not even as a child. It was fun…and arousing. Being so close to him, she could feel the heat emanating from him and smell his cologne. Her breasts were pressed tightly against his unyielding back. Anika bounced with each of his steps. Having her thighs wrapped around his hips allowed her core to make fleeting contact with him. The thin silk of her trousers offered little to separate them and his solid muscle rubbed against it and the lace of her panties creating a delicious friction.

Anika tried to adjust herself, to put some space between them, but Luca held her fast. Thwarted, she did her utmost to distract her overstimulated mind with the scenery. The buildings were definitely older and looked worn, especially when compared to the glitz of the new buildings nearer the water. He took them down a narrow alley that crawled with tourists and packed with racks of clothing and stalls of goods. She might have to get him to swing closer on their way back so she could get a better look.

What surprised her was that he took her to a tiny restaurant with faded red awning, smudges on the windows and a line of patrons winding down the street. It certainly wasn't what she'd been expecting. Luca stopped in front of one window and waved to catch the attention of a slight man with gray hair and friendly face who stood behind the counter. Luca was met with an immediate grin and a thumbs-up.

Order apparently made, he carried her to the wall then put her down so they could watch the street traffic side by side.

He angled his head to look at her with a satisfied grin. "Surprised?"

"Well, yeah. This doesn't seem like a place you would eat at." She looked up pointedly at the awning and the crowds of tourists. There wasn't a suit or tie in sight.

"Or is it somewhere *you* wouldn't eat?"

She wanted to bop him on the top of the head. He thought she was some sort of diva? Before she could reply, the same man from the window appeared with a plastic bag.

"Luca! It's about time you came for a visit!" He gave Luca a big hug. Over Luca's shoulder, he gave Anika a polite smile and curious glance. He stepped back and warmly smiled up at him as he handed him his small burden. "Your usual."

"Thanks, René." Luca handed him some cash, clapped him on the back and accepted the bag. "It's been too long since I've had one of these."

René looked over at Anika expectantly.

"Anika, René. He makes the best food in all of Nice."

The man burst out laughing and punched Luca on the shoulder. "He exaggerates. But I am not when I say you are breathtaking." He nodded at Luca. "It's about time."

Luca rolled his eyes in mock exasperation. "Don't you have a restaurant to run?"

"I do." He pressed a hand to her shoulder then Luca's "Come around more often, then. Both of you." The man winked at Anika and waved goodbye before rushing back to the bustling restaurant.

The savory scent coming from the bag had her licking her lips in anticipation. "So what is it?"

"It's called socca." He handed it to Anika, picked her up again and started walking. "It's a chickpea pancake with various toppings. It's delicious."

"It smells like it." Anika took a quick peek and smiled at what looked like a flat quiche that had been cut into slices like a pizza. "So where to now?"

"The perfect place to eat it, of course."

She could only imagine where that could be.

Luca strolled to a park that overlooked the beach. When he'd said to René that he hadn't been back in a while, it was the truth. It had been too long. Work had either kept him moving or stuck in boardrooms and office buildings. He couldn't remember the last time he'd walked along a beach, or driven along the coast. It was liberating.

He found an empty bench that faced the sunset and slowly lowered her to the ground. "Your table, milady."

Anika's laughter tinkled as she sat. Her eyes sparkled with delight when he opened the box and offered her a slice.

"You're going to love this."

Smiling, she took a bite. She dropped her head back, Anika groaned as she chewed. "You're right."

Delighted, he took a slice of his own then copied her. It was better than he remembered. René had even added a couple of bottles of soft drink. Luca made a mental note to visit his friend more often.

He smiled again when Anika reached for another slice. She took a delicate nibble then chewed thoughtfully as if she was trying to memorize the taste. Had she ever had anything so simple? He doubted it.

Luca handed her one of the bottles. "So you think you'll ever have this again?"

She took it with a smile. "Absolutely."

He couldn't help but be charmed when she wiped her mouth with the back of her hand before taking a swig of her drink.

"So how did you find out about that place anyway? It seems popular with the tourists, but I can't imagine you tripped over it accidentally."

The memory tugged something in his chest. "It's a long story."

"Oh." The smile faded from her face as she took another bite.

Luca slid his hand over her knee. "I don't mean to be short." He paused as he tried to put the words together. "It was a long time ago. A time I'd rather not remember."

"I'm sorry I brought it up."

Shaking his head, he forced a smile. "You didn't know." He scanned the scene around them and his smile turned genuine. Waving his hand, he motioned for some street performers to come closer. A guitarist and singer immediately launched into a song about two lovers in the night.

It didn't take them long to decimate the socca and wash it down with the drinks. Luca wiped his hands and stood, holding one out to her as he did.

She looked at him, puzzlement clear on her face as she obviously wondered what he had up his sleeve now. What made him smile was how when she had no idea what was to come, she still took his hand.

She trusted him — at least as far as taking his hand went — and that pleased him. He helped her to her feet then spun her into his arms so they could sway in time with the music.

The feel of being in his arms, dancing in the middle of a park, after having the closest thing she'd ever had to a picnic as they were serenaded by street performers — it was surreal — and impetuous and fun. Two words no one had ever used in conjunction with the name Anika De Winter. She was already dizzy before he spun her. Anika wasn't sure if it was because of the situation or the proximity to Luca. Perhaps it was both, but it was heady and intoxicating and it thrilled her — made her feel alive.

The tone of the music changed into the driving beat of a tango. The singer stood aside, swaying to the music, watching on as she allowed the guitar to take center stage.

Luca didn't miss a step, tugging her into an intimate embrace. He danced her around the little space as if it was something he did all the time. His movements were quick, sure, precise. Anika's head whirled as he spun her out, snapped her back in then dipped her, holding the dramatic pose as the melody faded away.

Breathless, she stared up at him. Luca's eyes were as dark as night, his mouth inches away from hers, his breath coming in short puffs against her cheek. She wanted to believe it was the way she was being held almost upside down that caused her light-headedness, but Anika couldn't fool herself.

It was Luca.

She snapped herself out of the trance and gave him a teasing smile, needing to put some space between them, even if it was just figuratively. "So the man can tango as well. Is there anything you can't do?"

He smiled and pulled her back up. "Don't ever ask me to sing, or cook anything more complicated than scrambled eggs and we won't have a problem."

Imagining him making her scrambled eggs for breakfast after a torrid night together muddled up her mind even more. Anika managed a laugh, although what she wanted to do was press herself up against him again. Sadly, Luca had paid the musicians so they had moved on. It was probably for the best.

"Shall we get back, then?" A small part of her hoped he would refuse her suggestion. That he would think of something else incredibly romantic for them to do.

A look at the horizon had her stopping to admire the beauty of the setting sun. It was still bright out, but the ribbons of color were starting to appear again. The sky blazed gold and orange at the moment, as if she was standing in the middle of masterfully cut citrine gemstone.

"I guess we should." He sounded genuinely disappointed that they had to return. He held out his hand. "Back along the beach?"

"Absolutely."

Chapter Five

The drive back along the Moyenne Corniche was just as spectacular as the drive there but, as he'd promised, this time she could really enjoy the vista. The winding roads carved into the cliff side added to the thrill of Luca's driving and the crash of the waves below.

Luca handled the car expertly, easily guiding it around the corners as if it was an extension of himself. It pleased her that this car belonged to someone who could handle it so well. There was nothing worse than something so beautiful — so well crafted — not used to its potential.

Anika let her gaze stay on the fingers of color fanning up from the horizon for a while. She was perfectly at ease with him behind the wheel. When she turned her attention to him, Anika saw the concentration under the calm, competent control. He drove with ferocity. Not that she expected anything less from him.

"You drive like a racer."

Her comment put a smile on his face. "What makes you think that?"

"The way you shift." She leaned as they whipped around a bend. "How you take the corners."

"You caught me. I've raced a few times in the European Rallycross." He spared her a quick glance. "How would you know how a racer drives?"

Anika was impressed. "How do you think I learned? I hired one to teach me."

Luca laughed. "That's the best way to learn."

Anika smiled, enjoying the happy, relaxed mood between them. "Do you still race?"

He shook his head with a frown. "Unfortunately, work keeps me too busy to prepare properly to compete."

At least he wasn't foolish enough to just jump into the competition and think he could just do it. So, Luca was a bit of a daredevil. He had to be to race Rallycross.

Still, she wondered about his past. The sadness in his eyes when she'd asked about the restaurant haunted her. What could have happened to him as a child that a memory could put that look on his face?

The sky had turned an inky blue by the time they pulled up to the gleaming hotel.

The valet appeared out of the foyer then rushed over and opened the door for Anika. Luca handed the keys over as he rounded the car. He swept an arm around her waist as they made their way into the building. She enjoyed his touch and wanted to lean farther into it, but stopped herself.

Luca paused in front of the desk but not before giving her a peck on the cheek. "I have something to take care of, but you should dress for a black tie affair."

His high-handedness amused her. "Oh, really?"

"Yes." He pecked her again. "I'll meet you shortly."

Anika rushed up to her room, showered, then as she got dressed, she did a quick search for Luca's younger years online. Nothing came up. No matter what terms she searched for, there were no results. It was as though he hadn't existed until he was already a multimillionaire. It puzzled her just as much as the man himself did.

So far, nothing they had done had met her expectations. Anika had imagined him to be the type of man who knew only extravagance and would use his money to dazzle her. Sure, his car cost more than most people made in a year, but everything else had been relatively low key. And it had been wonderful.

His reputation as a playboy led her to believe that he would only be interested in sex. And while she knew he wanted her — how could she not when the chemistry between them sparked whenever they were anywhere near each another — he seemed just as interested in spending time getting to know her.

Or, it could all be some elaborate game he was playing to amuse himself. Then again, wasn't that what she was doing with him? Luca Rossi was the best diversion she'd ever encountered.

The knock at the door startled her back to reality. Anika gave herself one last onceover. Her red silk dress was little more than a tailored sheath that fit like a second skin. She didn't know what possessed her to bring it when she'd never had the audacity to wear it even once before. Now she was glad she had. It contrasted wonderfully with her pale skin and dark hair. Thanks to the dedicated concierge service provided by Totally Five Star, all she had to do was ask and, like a magic genie, they provided everything she needed. A jeweler, a hair stylist and makeup artist all swept in, did their jobs and vanished just as quickly. As a result, she wore lipstick, nails and gems to match the dress. Even her upswept hair was held in place with a ruby-studded comb. She turned to look at the back of her dress as she exited the room. The plunging backline hadn't allowed for a bra, and if it skimmed just half an inch lower, she wouldn't have been able to wear panties, either.

Rather than cringe, Anika grinned. The liberation she felt just wearing the daring dress felt wonderful.

Her self-confidence skyrocketed when she opened the door and Luca's eyes rounded a split second before he let them roam hungrily over her body. "You look fantastic."

She could say the same about him. He looked like James Bond's darker and more dangerous brother in the finely cut black tux. "You clean up well yourself."

He laughed and offered his arm. Anika grabbed her new clutch from the table then linked her arm through his. "So black tie, huh?"

"I thought since we're here, we might as well pretend to fit in with the glitterati."

So he didn't feel like he fit in either. If he acted as he had that afternoon on a daily basis, it was no wonder. Then again, she did her best to do what was expected of her and she still didn't feel like she fell into any particular role. Like an oval peg trying to fit into a round hole. Almost fit but just didn't despite looking the part.

They wandered through the sleepy hotel like a couple in love. No rush. No real destination. Just two people enjoying their time together. Their meandering stroll took them along a different path through the building. As difficult as it was to tear her attention away from Luca, she couldn't help but notice the opulence of the hotel. They ended up farther in the building at a crossroads of sorts. Discreet signs pointed to archways leading to the spa, the pool and so on. But Anika couldn't stop staring at the magnificent fountain that misted the air from its dominant space at the center of the room.

The glass dome overhead filtered the moonlight as it played with the water, turning the droplets into diamonds cascading over the marble. The construct itself was quite plain compared to the other fountains she'd seen in the city, but it didn't need any augmentation to make it any more magical.

A silvery glint from the water at the base caught her eye. Anika stepped closer, although she knew the mist would play havoc with her hair and makeup. She gasped with delight at the silvery fish rushing to and fro in the shallow pool. Beneath them, she spied the shine of coins.

"Would you like to make a wish?" Luca held up a coin.

Smiling, Anika shrugged. "I wouldn't know what to wish for. I have just about everything any woman could want in life. Asking for more just seems greedy."

He chuckled. "I know the feeling. Though, the ancients believed that water from fountains was a gift from the gods for which they demanded a token of gratitude in return." He lowered his voice conspiratorially and leaned in close to whisper, "We wouldn't want to offend the gods now, would we?"

He stepped back far too soon for her liking. Luca's gaze held hers as he pressed the coin gently to her lips, then his, before tossing it over his shoulder into the water.

Enchanted, Anika watched as the coin hit the surface with a little splash and it drifted to the bottom through the darting fish.

"Come." Luca wound his arm around her waist and led her through the arch leading to reception.

Marie-Thérèse stood behind the desk and nodded to them in greeting as they walked past. The formerly bright lighting had been dimmed, adding to the romance of the atmosphere. It couldn't get any more dreamlike unless they lit the room with candlelight.

Eventually, they made it outside into the cool night air. The whisper of a breeze coaxed goosebumps over her arms.

Luca noticed immediately and rubbed his hands lightly over her skin as he led her toward the waiting limo. Any chill evaporated instantly in the fiery wake of his touch. He helped her into the back of the long, shining car then slid in beside her. A couple of knocks on the ceiling with his hand, and they were off.

This time Anika didn't mind his nearness. In fact, she wanted to get closer. She looked up at him to gauge what was going on in his head but found him already watching her intently. "You truly are beautiful."

Words she had heard before but this time they rung with the truth. Her heart buoyed to beat in her throat, blocking out any words — not that she could formulate a sentence at the moment. Instead, she pressed her mouth to his, wanting to silence and taste him all at once.

Luca instantaneously pulled her against him, tugging her over him until she was almost flat on her back in his lap. He parted her mouth with a skillful move of his lips, easing hers open, and teasing her with lazy strokes of his tongue.

Anika wrapped her arms around his neck, clawing her nails in his hair, holding him tightly. She pulled back long enough to command, "Touch me."

He responded quickly, gliding one hand up her side, sliding slowly up the silk to cup her breast.

The heat of his hand through the thin fabric coaxed her nipple to a hard point that pressed eagerly into his palm. Anika arched into it, delighting in the sensation streaking through her. Luca rolled her under him, taking advantage of the new position to use both his hands to touch her as she'd instructed. He used one to continue caressing her breast while the other slowly he slid down her leg to the hem of her dress. Once there, he danced his fingers around her ankle, eliciting more sparks of sensation. Who knew it could be so sensitive?

He dragged his fingers up her bare legs, taking the fabric up with him. The cool air and heat of his touch mingled on her skin. She gasped against his mouth. The confusing mix only heightened her pleasure.

Luca ground his hardened cock against her, the friction exciting her even more, building the tension ever growing inside her until she thought she would explode. Until she wanted to explode.

"Luca, please."

He slid his fingers over her clit through her panties. Anika lurched against him. The sensation was powerful, all-consuming.

"Do I have your permission to slide my fingers inside you?"

Anika writhed against him mindlessly. "Yes." *Anything.*

Luca asked, "And to use them to fuck you until you come screaming in my lap?"

God, yes. Anika held his gaze as she nodded vehemently. "Please."

It was all he needed to hear.

Luca wrenched aside the lace and eased two fingers into her passion-slicked slit. She squeezed her legs together against the squelching movement of his hand. He wedged his knees between hers to pry them apart, leaving her open for the sensual assault of his fingers.

With every pump of his fingers and graze of the heel of his hand against her clit, Anika's body wound tighter and tighter until all the sensations collided and exploded.

Dazedly, she stared at his face. The intense look in his eyes, the clench of his jaw, had her convinced his control was about to snap then he would tear their clothes off and he would take her right there in the back of the limo.

And she wouldn't do a thing to stop him.

Sadly, the car slowed to a stop. Moments later, the driver's door opened and closed. Just a breath before there was a discreet knock at the door.

Anika gave Luca a slightly panicked look but he kissed it away. He helped her back into her seat, chuckling as she hurried to right her hair and her dress. "Relax. He has no idea what's been going on back here."

"I think he might when he sees the state of us." She glared archly at his hair and the lipstick staining his mouth.

He ran his fingers through his hair and pulled out a handkerchief to mitigate the damage to his face.

Anika extracted a hand mirror from her clutch and quickly refreshed her lipstick and did her best to fix her hair.

Luca rolled his eyes and yanked the comb from her hair, letting it tumble over her shoulders in ebony waves. "Much better."

If it had been anyone else, she might have had a minor fit at him for ruining the effort that had been put into the hairstyle. Only with Luca, it seemed so simple. She couldn't fix it, so the logical thing to do was leave it down. No muss. No fuss. She ran her fingers through it then tossed the comb into her purse.

He took her hands, tugging so she looked him in the eyes. "You're beautiful. Every man will be jealous of me tonight."

When he said things like that, she had to wonder how many women he's said the very same thing to in the past? Did he make them all feel as special as he did her?

The notion dampened her mood a little. That was until she exited the limo and glanced up the grand stairs at the building brilliantly illuminated like a gleaming beacon in the night.

The Casino de Monte Carlo.

Luca watched as her face lit up. Something on her mind had caused her to drift away from him for a moment, but the instant her attention turned to the magnificent architecture of the casino, it had been forgotten. The brief, lost look in her eyes hollowed his stomach. He preferred her smiling and carefree as she had been during their trip to Nice. After seeing the vibrant woman beneath the cool façade he would make sure that the cold aloof Ice Princess never again reappeared.

Only he had to work slowly if it was going to happen. And it would probably take a little sharing on his part as well. When she'd asked him about his past, he hadn't been prepared. No one had asked him before. People tended to focus on his money and what he could do for them. Luca hadn't known how to respond to an honest question about *him*. He didn't intend for her to be in his life long enough to wonder, and yet she had. And when he rebuffed her, he'd hurt her.

He had to proceed cautiously when it came to matters that went beyond slaking his lust. In that case, she wanted him just as much as he wanted her. The day had truly been enjoyable. She surprised him with her skill behind a wheel as well as how easily she had adapted, eating food she'd never tried before, on a park bench no less. The feel of her against him as they'd danced had intoxicated him. It would have been so easy to believe that they truly were lovers enjoying a little trip together.

Luca reminded himself of his self-imposed rules. He wouldn't let her under his skin. She was beautiful, yes, but he'd been with gorgeous women before. This relationship would last only the weekend. No more.

Anika turned to him with a childlike smile on her face and he felt his heart crack a little. "Have you ever gambled here?"

She blushed, and he found it adorable.

"I watched a…friend lose a bundle here, if that's what you're asking. I've never actually played myself."

"We shall remedy that tonight." He wound an arm around her waist, and they entered the casino.

Just like every building in Monaco, the casino was extravagantly decorated to the max. The patrons dripped with jewels and designer clothing, adding to the opulence of the place. It wasn't his style, but it worked for this city. It was all about decadence, obvious excess. He liked to think himself more discreet. He liked fine things. He worked hard enough for them but he didn't feel the need to flaunt them.

Yet today, he'd made sure Anika knew he had an extravagant supercar. He didn't know what possessed him to let her get behind the wheel. That turned out to be a pleasant surprise — and a huge turn-on.

He couldn't wait to see what else she had hidden — especially what was under her clothes.

Luca forced his mind away from getting her naked lest he embarrass them both. He led them through the magnificent foyer. The marble floors and massive pillars shone under the radiant chandeliers. Above them, the arches and stained-glass ceiling added to the grandeur of the lobby. The woman at the podium smiled and waved him through, earning a surprised look from Anika. He shrugged and led the way into the first room, La Salle Europe. The gilded ceiling and crystal chandeliers granted the room a golden glow, lighting the tables and the many patrons.

He smiled at his companion and waved toward the room. "What would you like to play?"

She looked at him, her brilliant sapphire eyes wide. "I have no idea. Gambling isn't my vice."

"I guess we'll just have to see what catches your eye."

That was just it. *Everything* caught her eye. They wandered for a while in companionable silence. Anika absorbed the ambiance, enjoying the extravagance of the casino. The scent of expensive perfume mingled with something unique in the air to create a pungent aroma that wasn't entirely unpleasant. Her sharp eyes caught De Winter gemstones on many of the women's throats, fingers and wrists that made her smile even more.

Pleased to see that the latest PR campaign had hit the right demographic, she let Luca lead the way through the throngs of designer suits and glamorous couture.

Anika stood a little taller knowing they were noticed. She saw the glances Luca received from almost all the women. The ones that seemed immune by his looks were either blind or were too engrossed in their games to care. Their gazes prickled her skin. Coerced the hair on the back of her neck stand on end. After living most of her life under the scrutiny of others, she wanted nothing more than to go back to her hotel room and hide. But what bothered her the most was that they wanted the man next to her. A covetous little voice at the back her mind screamed at her to remind them whom he belonged to. To mark her territory. She shoved the inane thought aside. He wasn't hers to mark.

Luca curled a hand around hers. Had he noticed her discomfort? It wouldn't surprise her if he had. The man missed nothing. But could he see past her practiced icy veneer after knowing each other for such a short time?

As if to confirm her suspicions, he winked and gave her a wicked smile that sent shivers cascading down her spine. He leaned in, his lips a breath away from her earlobe. The spice of his cologne wound its way around her as tangible as his arms. "They are nothing. Don't let them see that you care."

Wasn't that just the motto of her life? Adopting a cat-that-got-the-cream smile, she tilted her head back to look up at him. "So what do you suggest I do?"

"Enjoy yourself. Forget about the prying eyes." He brushed his lips against hers. "You might even have a little fun."

The small gesture sent ripples of reaction throughout the room. Though he adopted a don't-care attitude, he must have noticed. But taking his own advice, he didn't react whatsoever, as he found a space for them at the baccarat table.

Anika shook it off, applying her focus on learning to play the game. Luca talked her through the rules, making it simple to understand. Within the hour, they were friendly rivals. Luca won often, but when he didn't, he lost graciously, even though the number of zeroes he'd relinquished would have made most men weep.

The first hand she won was a rush of adrenaline. No wonder gambling was addictive. Wide-eyed and breathless, she bet again. Anika won twice more before she called it quits. Relinquishing her seat, she took a place behind Luca and watched as the other players upped their bets to astronomical sums without batting an eyelash. Luca was among them, goading on his competitors with his cocky attitude and confident smile.

What made her most curious was whenever he won a large sum, he would wave a little man over and sign something before the man would scurry away again. What was he up to?

She tried to peek at what he signed the next time he waved the man over, but a touch on her arm drew her attention away at the last second.

"Anika, what a surprise to see you here, darling."

The older woman was bedecked in De Winter's latest line, though in far too much of it in Anika's eyes. Not that she was complaining. It just looked gaudy. She preferred a sparkle here and there rather than dripping head to toe in jewels. In her mind, when anyone wore enough gems to blind bystanders, it came across as trying too hard.

"How nice to see you, Camilla." It truly wasn't. Of all the people she had to run into, it had to be the woman known in her circles as The Mouth.

The It girl from decades past, she now made it her business to know everyone else's business. Word that Anika was in Monaco with Luca would spread faster than it would on the Internet.

"I was so sorry to hear about your wedding, though I was a bit hurt that I hadn't been invited." She pouted her too pink lips.

"I was the one hurt when I saw you weren't there." Anika kept the smile frozen on her lips. "I'm sure the invitation simply got lost in the mail. I can't imagine getting married without you present."

"Well, you didn't marry, so all's well that ends well."

Anika couldn't believe that the only thing the woman cared about was herself, although it was better than hearing false condolences and platitudes about how things would get better. Or how she hadn't found the right man yet.

"So, who are you here with so soon after your failed nuptials?" She craned her head to get a look at Luca. When she returned her gaze to Anika, her eyes sparkled with delight. "My, my. Luca Rossi. You do work fast, my dear."

Anika bristled at the tone the woman's voice took. It didn't matter that she wanted exactly what the woman implied they were doing. "Luca and I just met, actually. We thought since we were both here alone we'd…keep each other company."

Camilla patted her stark white hair. Anika could see her ferreting the information away for later. The woman practically buzzed with delight.

Luca stood then, towering over them both. He took Camilla's hand and kissed the back of it. "Mrs. Chamberlain, how nice to see you again."

His tone said otherwise, but Camilla seemed oblivious. It seemed his charm worked on her incredibly well.

She tried to fan the flush from her cheeks with her free hand, apparently in no hurry to release his grip just yet. "I was just relaying my condolences to Anika regarding the to-do of her marriage falling through, but I see now that my concern was misplaced."

"Her fiancé was a fool. Or perhaps he simply realized he was too obtuse for her. In either case, she's better off without him." Luca shrugged and smiled at Anika. "His loss is my gain."

Camilla opened and closed her mouth, yet she couldn't seem to find the words to reply to his statement.

Luca smiled and nodded. "Now, if you'll excuse us. We have an obscene amount of money to try to lose."

And with that, he swept Anika past the still-gaping Camilla.

Anika trembled at his side. Furious at the gossiping old hag and wanting nothing more than to comfort Anika, Luca shielded her as they wove through the mass of people until they were once again outside.

It wasn't until they were at the fountains that he stopped to look at her, willing to do whatever it took to coax a smile to her face. When he sat her on the edge of the nearest fountain and knelt in front of her, he noted her shaking shoulders. He slid the jacket from his shoulders and wrapped it around hers.

Then she looked up at him with a big grin on her face. Anika hadn't been crying at all. She'd been laughing the whole time.

The tightness in his gut relaxed and his breath came easier. "You little minx. I thought you were in true emotional distress."

"Sorry," she managed to gasp between giggles.

"I'm glad you were able to find the humor in her barbs." He sighed. Her smile was contagious. He quickly found his own mouth beginning to curve upward. "That woman is a real harridan."

"I know. She's been a frequent guest at my parents' parties for years. She drives everyone bonkers."

Luca looked at Anika. "Her words truly didn't bother you?"

"Not really. I've been dealing with people like her my whole life." Anika smiled at him. "That was just so strange."

"What was so strange about it if you're used to people like her?"

The flush on her cheeks heightened. "You're the first person to come to my rescue."

He stared at her. "You're not serious."

"It's not like I need rescuing. I can handle myself. You're just the first to ever take it upon himself to try and help me out." She took his hand. "So thank you for that."

No one had ever stood up for her? He found that hard to believe. The urge to give her whatever she wanted, to protect her, was like breathing. At least it was to him. He wanted to give her whatever she wished for. It was an inclination that was beginning to concern him.

He shook it off. Anika was a novelty. He would soon get over her, especially once he got her under him.

Tonight. He would bed her then, if he was still inclined, the rest of the weekend would be spent in bed as well. Once Monday came along, all would be right with the world again and he could get on with his life.

What would that be like? He'd known Anika for twenty-four hours and he couldn't stop thinking about her. He didn't want to stop thinking about her. That was the frightening thing. He wanted to see what Anika looked like first thing in the morning. Wondered what she looked like in the rain. He even wondered what she would look like when the ice cracked and the fire of her anger blasted through. Most of all, he wanted to see what she looked like in the afterglow of making love.

The thought was incredibly arousing. He wanted her — now. "Are you up for a walk?"

"I am." She let him help her up. "So what else is on the agenda for today?"

"I don't know." And he didn't. All he knew was that he needed to get her into bed before he lost his mind completely. "Let's see where our feet take us."

"Sounds good." Anika liked the lack of planning. The idea of just wandering aimlessly usually would have sounded like a complete waste of time, but after the day they'd had, she looked forward to it. Who knew what they would end up doing?

They walked toward the water then along the harbor front. Like everything else in Monaco, the quay gleamed golden in the darkness. The string of lights outlined the docks and winked off the shining yachts as they bobbed in the serene water.

She gazed at the darkly handsome man next to her. "Can I ask you something?"

He crinkled his eyebrows wryly. "Depends on what you're asking."

"What were you signing in the casino?"

She caught the quick quirk of his lips.

"It was nothing."

"I think it was something." She shrugged. "But you don't have to tell me if you don't want."

The small curve grew into an impressed smile. "You're quite observant."

"I like to think so." Was he going to open up to her? His amenable smile certainly got her hopes up. He was enigmatic, which was appealing on its own level, but she wanted to know more about him.

He waited a little while before answering. "I sign over big winnings to a charity. A children's charity with the aim of getting kids off the streets and situated somewhere safe."

He said it like it was nothing.

"That's wonderful." She stared at him for a little while.

"But…" He smiled expectantly.

She cocked her head with a shrug. "Most men would be shouting it from the rooftops. Or at least make it obvious to the women they're with."

"I don't do it for the recognition." Luca shrugged and leaned closer. "Or to impress women."

That made her laugh.

His warm breath grazed her cheek when he said, "Besides, it would ruin my reputation."

He was too close and it was scrambling her brains. The air crackled between them as she tried to put some space between them.

Anika took a deep breath of the salted sea air and sighed as she took in the scenery, looking for anything to distract herself from the man next to her. "So which one of those is yours?"

He looked at her questioningly, even though she could see a hint of a smirk forming at the corners of his sensuous mouth.

"What makes you think I have a boat?"

"I just have a hunch."

He grinned. "Let's play a game, then. See if you can guess. With each wrong guess, you'll owe me a forfeit."

"And just what might that be?"

"A kiss."

It piqued her interest. She liked to think that she was a good judge of character. It would simply be a matter of reconciling the man with his boat. If his taste in cars were anything to go by, it wouldn't be too hard to figure out. And if the worst thing she had to give up was a kiss, she wouldn't mind being incorrect once or twice. Not that she would. "Deal."

Anika studied Port Hercule and immediately disregarded the smaller vessels. A man like Luca would prefer grand ships to the little boats, so those were out. The biggest ones seemed too obvious, but she kept a couple in mind because they seemed to be something he would like. So far, she knew he wasn't prone to showing off...too much. He had enough money to buy just about every yacht in the marina several times over. He liked fast cars and, according to the online reports, he liked sexy women.

"That one." She pointed to the sleek yacht bobbing next to the biggest she could see.

"Nope." He didn't give her a chance to register that she'd made a mistake. Luca cupped her cheeks and brushed his lips against hers. "Try again."

Though the touch had been slight, Anika's body started humming in response. If she wasn't careful, she could easily lose her head, which meant losing the bet, and that just wouldn't do.

Blinking a few times to refocus her eyes, she studied the water again. "The sporty one over there." She pointed to the far side of the pier. "Near the hideous one that looks like a trawler."

"Guess again." This time is hand tunneled into the hair at the back of her head to cradle her as he slowly plundered her lips. When he pulled back, her breath came in short pants.

Focus took longer to regain, but Anika glared at the water, sure she could figure it out. "The Sunseeker with *Passion* on the side."

"You would think, but no." He fit her body against his, cupping her bottom, pressing her intimately against him, this time kissing his way up the slender column of her throat on his way to her lips.

Hearing only the rushing of blood in her ears, she gasped another attempt. "The Benetti…"

"No."

Stubbornly, she persisted although the words she uttered were barely a whisper. "Which one?"

Anika was glad he was wound around her as he was, because she didn't think her knees would hold out much longer. Clinging to him now, she rubbed herself against the hard, unyielding lines of his body. The thick bulge of his erection pressed against her insistently while he ruthlessly probed her mouth with his tongue, driving out any sane thought.

"Does it matter?"

Anika didn't care that they were in the middle of Monte Carlo Harbor pawing at each other like teens. She didn't care about winning. She only wanted him — now.

"No."

His eyes were dark when he finally drew back and looked down at her. The tension came off his body in waves and she knew he was having trouble containing himself as well.

He lowered his head to kiss her again. Hard and biting, it stole the breath from her lungs. Gentle persuasion was long forgotten it seemed, as he ran his hands over her. He slid one on a confident path down her spine, under her dress and panties to grip the curve of her bottom, pressing her against him unapologetically.

Anika arched into the palm of his other hand as he found his way under the fabric to cup her breast. She barely managed to stifle the moan he teased from her when he flicked his thumb over the hard peak.

Apparently getting his hands on her wasn't enough. Pressing her against the wall, he found a better use for them and hefted her against the stone, bringing her breasts level with his mouth. A change in position he used to his benefit. Nuzzling the material aside, Luca closed his hot, moist mouth over one aching nipple, sucking and licking like a man starved.

She clawed her nails into his head to hold him close, unwilling to let him stop the exquisite laving of his tongue. Luca continued to torture her sensuously as he secured her with one arm. With the other free, he rucked her dress up so he could have access to her. Luca only had to brush his thumb over her lace-covered clit a few times before she unraveled in his arms with a silent cry.

As Anika came down from her orgasm, she felt the tension running through Luca. He trembled as he fought for control of himself. She cupped his cheeks, kissing him, running her tongue over his lips letting him know she wanted him.

He searched her eyes for a moment before coming to a silent conclusion. She knew what he was thinking, because she'd made up her mind in the same instant.

Luca dropped her to her feet and allowed her a second to right her clothes before he snared her hand and led her back up the sidewalk.

It took a few blurred minutes to arrive back at the hotel, though it seemed like eons. Anika was only dimly aware of rushing through the lobby and the dizzying ride in the elevator before they reached the penthouse suite.

The elevator opened into an alcove in the opulent living space. Like her own suite, it was filled with perfectly chosen furniture and accompanying accents. Only it was much bigger. Luca kept hold of her hand as he led her to the balcony doors. He deftly opened the French doors one at a time and tugged her through the softly billowing curtains.

He pressed his lips to hers once again — tasting her. He licked his lips when he drew back. Even in the dim light she could see the desire in his eyes.

"I want you, Anika. I want you spread under me crying out my name. But I want to do this right." He leveled his dark gaze on hers, looking for understanding.

Curious to see what he would do next, Anika nodded. She needed a second to catch her breath.

"Make yourself at home. I'm going to make a call to room service." After one last hard kiss on her lips, he pulled his phone out of his jacket pocket and strode into the room.

Running her fingers over the fluttering pulse at her neck, she turned to stare at the view. Did the hotel do anything other than stunning scenery? The water glittered under the pale moonlight like a masterfully cut gem. She inhaled the salty sea air and willed herself to calm down.

Only she couldn't. How could she? She and Luca were going to have sex and the thought alone was enough to send her blood pressure soaring.

Exploring his suite seemed like a reasonable way of distracting herself.

The penthouse looked almost like hers, except on a larger scale. The ceiling was much higher and as a result, the windows were so large it gave the illusion of nothing separating the room from the darkness outside. Illuminating the room from above with soft diffused light was another massive chandelier. It was amazing how many of them graced the hotel and yet were all different from one another. This one was designed to look like floating crystals. Anika liked it enough to consider looking into having one installed in her apartment once she got back.

She walked past the staircase to the upper level as she took in the details of the room.

On one wall, hung a huge flat-screen TV that would give some theaters a run for their money. Across the way, behind a grand piano, a fireplace graced the lower portion of a wall under what looked like an original Klimt.

Luca spoke quietly on the phone in the kitchen as he paced back and forth. He caught her eye. Anika felt the heat of his gaze from across the room. He held up a finger, indicating he would only be a moment more. She nodded and resumed her tour. Another floating crystal chandelier drifted above the twelve-chaired table in the dining room. The hall led to a huge, modern office, a marble and glass bathroom complete with massive tub and separate shower and two luxuriously decorated bedrooms that rivaled her own bedroom at home.

By the time she made her way back to the living area, Luca had put away the phone.

Not knowing what to expect, her stomach fluttered as she approached him.

"My order should be arriving momentarily." He took her hand when she came within arm's reach and drew her close. "Are you okay?"

Anika nodded. "Fine." She knew she hadn't convinced him. He would have to be insensate not to see the tremble in her hand or hear the tremor in her voice.

He pressed her palm to his lips, caressing the skin there with a gentle brush of his mouth. "I know how you feel. I want this as much as you do. I just want to take our time. We have all night. There's no need to rush."

Except she felt like she was going to burst out of her skin at the slightest provocation.

Anika jumped a little when there was a knock at the door.

Luca smiled and released her hand to answer. Moments later, he returned with a cart. She spied a bottle of Cristal in a sweating ice bucket and something hidden beneath a small silver dome.

"Take the tray, Anika." Luca had already picked up the bucket and a pair of champagne glasses prepared with plump strawberries at their bottoms.

She did as he'd asked. It was light and easily carried as she followed him.

Luca strode straight for the staircase and up them without pause.

Anika had an inkling of what she would find when she reached the top, but the sight of the master bedroom took her breath away. The entire upper level was a single room except for a couple of doors, one of which she assumed led to a bathroom. There was no wall to block the view of the windows or the living area below.

But it was the bed dominating the space that drew her focus. The sumptuous, light-colored bedding and piles of thick pillows gave it the appearance of a cloud pulled together for their enjoyment. She had no doubt that it would be as soft as it looked.

And that she would soon find out.

Anika turned back to stare out of the window.

"You're not afraid of heights, are you?" Luca dexterously popped the cork and poured the fizzing liquid into the glasses before putting them aside on the railing.

"Not at all. Just admiring the view." She held out the tray, curious about what the dome hid.

Luca smiled as he lifted the covering to reveal a bowl of black cherries still on the stem. Each one had been dipped in white chocolate and adorned with little silver beads that she assumed were decorative sugar. They almost winked enticingly in the light.

He hadn't failed to surprise her.

Anika grinned at Luca. "Not chocolate-dipped strawberries?"

"A cliché," he chuckled. Luca handed her one of the glasses before he picked up a cherry by its stem and held it in front of her lips. "Try it."

Anika grasped it between her teeth and pulled it from the stem. It had been pitted and the slightly sharp flavor of the cherry mingled with the cloying sweetness of the chocolate perfectly. The sugar beads added texture with each bite completing a deliciously decadent treat.

"What do you think?"

"I've never had anything like it." She picked one up and held it out for him the same way he had for her.

Luca slowly drew the little berry into his mouth with an exaggerated curl of his tongue. He burst the fruit with an audible pop as he closed his eyes and chewed. Anika's breath hitched at his appreciative moan.

"They taste almost as good as you." Luca opened his eyes and let them drift to her straining nipples.

In an attempt to alleviate the sudden dryness of her mouth, Anika picked up a glass and took a long sip of champagne. The bubbles tickled her nose and burst on her tongue as she let the flavors of the cherry, chocolate, champagne and hint of strawberry mingle there.

"Nervous?" The soft caress of Luca's voice drew her attention to the fact he observed her closely.

She released a breath. "A little." The combination of nerves, anticipation and arousal left her jittery and more than a little lightheaded.

"Perhaps we should leave these for later." He took the glass from her and put it next to his on the railing.

The brush of his hand against hers raised goosebumps on her skin.

He circled behind her. She felt his touch through the thin fabric of her dress as if his fingers were tipped with flames. He slid his hands up her arms to cup her shoulders momentarily before he pushed the silk off them. Her dress slipped down her body with a whisper to pool at her feet. With her breasts bared to him, Luca wasted no time cupping them both, pressing urgent kisses on her shoulders and neck as he toyed with them. Gentle caresses alternated between less gentle pinches and tugs on her nipples.

Anika cried out as the slight pain from his treatment created an aching heat between her thighs. She hooked her arms around his neck to keep herself upright and to make sure his mouth stayed on her.

As if he knew what he was doing to her, Luca trailed one of his hands down over her stomach, tracing a lazy path to the silk of her panties. He followed the line back and forth, slowly, until she wanted to cry out from frustration. Clawing his hair finally got the result she wanted. He dipped his hand under the silk and eased his fingers between her legs to find her aching clit.

He knew exactly where to put his fingers, the right pressure, the perfect rhythm. After an entire day of what was essentially foreplay, it took seconds for him to bring her to a screaming climax. Luca muffled her exclamations with his hand. It surprised her — as she came down — that it turned her on to have him restrict her natural inclination. It aroused her more. Adding to the moisture building between her thighs.

Luca picked her up and, within seconds, placed her on the bed. When he stood up, Anika lurched upright. He wasn't going to leave her there, surely.

"Don't move."

Anika obeyed the curt demand only propping herself up on her elbows so she could see what he was doing. Luca had removed his jacket and was in the middle of undoing his tie. Anika watched, enraptured by his sure movements. He went to work on his shirtsleeves next, pulling out the cufflinks and placing them on the dresser. He rolled the sleeves up three turns each as he watched her with his penetrating eyes.

Anika could almost feel his glances on her skin. She didn't want almost. "Luca, please."

He opened the dresser and pulled out two ties. "Patience."

Her heart leaped in her chest. Was he really going to do what she thought? He walked closer, the ties dangling from his hand.

"Do I have your permission to use these on you?"

Anika nodded, squirming slightly on the duvet. She was willing to let him do almost anything if she could feel his skin against hers.

"Have you ever been tied up before?"

She hesitated a moment too long, because his expression shuttered and his hands dropped to his side. Anika quickly shook her head. "The truth is, I've never done…anything…with anyone before."

It was as though all the air was sucked out of the room. Luca let the ties fall from his fingers and slither to the floor. She was a virgin? And she wanted to be with him? He was humbled and incredibly aroused at the same time. "You're sure you want this? With me?"

"I've never been surer of anything."

No reply could have pleased him more. "I'll take care of you."

"I know."

Such trust in him. Luca would make sure it wasn't misplaced. "Come here."

She shimmied over the bed to sit on the edge in front of him.

He noticed earlier that she'd liked it when he'd covered her mouth to stifle her cries and she took commands without question. It would have been a pleasure to spread her on the bed, tie her down and bring her to orgasm after orgasm before finding his own gratification. But a virgin needed time, patience.

He should have said no. Being a woman's first was a big responsibility. She would remember him always. That thought was appealing to Luca. To be imprinted on her mind like she was on his. He would make it something worth remembering.

"Stand up."

She did as she'd been told.

Luca tugged her gently forward. "You are lovely." And she was. Standing in front of him in nothing but her gems, a wisp of silk between her thighs and heels on her feet, he would have expected her to be shy, but Anika stood straight and proud, eager for his gaze, his touch. He wouldn't disappoint her. But first, he wanted to see just how well she took instruction.

"Spread your legs."

Anika widened her stance. Her focus stayed on his eyes the entire time.

Pleased, he circled her. Close enough to bring goosebumps of awareness to her skin but without touching. "I want you to touch yourself."

On that, she hesitated. "I…"

He arched an eyebrow. "Don't know what to do?" She wasn't *that* innocent, surely.

Thankfully, she shook her head. "Where do you want me to start?"

Luca smiled. "Wherever feels right to you."

Anika gave him a wicked smile as she wound her fingers into her hair. She let her eyes drift closed while she toyed with it and she guided her other hand downward. She glided it over her neck and traced her collarbone while the other brushed her lips. Two fingers stroked her bottom lip once, twice, before she licked them delicately. Teasing the tips with her tongue, she smiled at him before sucking them deep.

Luca's cock twitched as if she had just taken it in her mouth instead of her fingers. Gritting his teeth, he stayed rooted to the spot, wanting to see what she else would do.

She let her free hand wander lower to circle the small mound of one breast. Her fingers spiraled ever inward until she reached her nipple. The soft gasp that escaped her when she gently pinched and tugged it had an immediate reaction on his body. Blood shot to his groin hardening him further, almost painfully.

Anika continued to drag her hand over her smooth, pale skin, letting it skate over the concave of her stomach before changing direction and curving over her hip and sliding over her thigh. Anika pulled her fingers partway out of her mouth. Giving them one final flick of her tongue, she slid them down between her breasts then slowly circled her navel before skating under the band of her panties.

Luca's mouth watered. Her movements were slow and deliberate as she pleasured herself. He watched closely, noting her motions, learning what she liked. Now he wanted to know what she looked like when she climaxed. He growled, "Make yourself come."

Anika opened her eyes then, leveling her incredibly blue gaze on him. She delved her fingers into her wet slit with determination, cupping herself, rocking her palm against her clit. Anika quivered, straining to find release. The room filled with her soft breaths, her sighs and the delicate squish of her fingers as she pumped them in and out of herself. The scent of her arousal spiced the air deliciously. It took seconds before he saw her eyes glaze over. Her focus on him grew fuzzy, but she kept her eyes open, riveted on his, as she cried out and trembles wracked her slender frame.

Luca caught her as her knees wobbled and she threatened to topple over. He had never been so aroused and wasted no time in getting her back on the bed. He took her shoes off then slipped off her panties. Luca then brushed his mouth along her legs, kissing a path upward. He parted her thighs, kissing the tender flesh of her folds.

Anika writhed beneath him as he lapped at her. He used his lips, tongue and even his breath to devastating effect. She'd read novels where heroes ravished the heroine, but she never imagined how incredible the sensations a man could invoke could be. What Luca was able to do to her was mind scrambling. She understood now why some people became so smitten with each other. Why people gave up everything for someone else. It was addictive. Luca was like a drug.

And they hadn't even reached actually having sex yet.

Muscles, in her arms, her abdomen, her thighs and deeper within, wound tighter and tighter until she thought she would explode. And still, with each exquisite lash of his tongue, she flew higher. Luca sucked and licked like a man starved. The rhythm of his movements drove her over the edge. Her second orgasm stunned her more than the first. Streaks of pleasure rushed through her as she convulsed under his masterful ministrations. He didn't stop until he wrung every last bit of sensation from her, and she had to push him away from her over-sensitized clit. It was too much. Too incredible. He was incredible.

She floated on a cloud of bliss for a while, dimly aware of Luca moving over her. Cell by cell, she became aware of his body hot and heavy on hers. He peered into her eyes as if he was trying to see into her soul.

"Are you okay?"

There were no words to describe what she was feeling. Anika nodded and wound her arms around his neck. Impatient, she shifted under him only stopping when his engorged cock slid into place against her slit. He was so big. A stab of fear chilled her.

Luca cupped her cheek. "I've taken care of protection."

She nodded, though his words did nothing to allay her fears.

"I have a feeling this will be a very tight fit, but if you're relaxed we shouldn't have a problem."

"Easy for you to say." Her voice shook and she hated that. What a time for her to show anxiety.

It didn't last long. Luca's hands and mouth were an immediate distraction. The feel of his hard body, skin to skin with hers at last, was sublime. She tentatively ran her hands over the hard angles of his shoulders and arms. At his pleased smile, she tried to venture farther but couldn't. He tipped them to their sides allowing her the freedom to explore his hard pecs and abs. He was beautiful.

Anika hesitated to travel farther downward, but Luca took her hand and guided her to his jutting erection. He pressed his lips against the sensitive hollow under her ear, as he whispered, "No shyness. We're about to become very well acquainted. You should be able to touch me freely."

She closed her hand experimentally around him. Anika couldn't quite get her fingers to touch, something that caused her eyes to widen slightly. He was huge and hard underneath smooth, hot skin. She slid her hand upward to the head, her confidence growing when his eyes fell closed and he groaned. He thrust his hips forward to slide himself in her grip.

She loved the power that surged through her. She had such control over a big, virile man like Luca. Anika lay back. There was only a slight tremor in her hands when she tugged him back over her. "Luca, I need you. Now."

He kissed her then. It was long, hot and deep. Luca nipped her bottom lip when he drew back to look her in the eyes.

She felt him against her then he pushed the big head inside her. Luca gripped her hips and surged forward. He worked his body into hers with small thrusts, gaining depth inch by inch. He held himself still once he filled her completely, giving her a chance to get used to his invasion.

Awed, Anika peered blindly up at him. There was so much sensation. Taut around his rigid girth, she was stuffed to bursting. Shifting under him, she sought to ease the ache and succeeded in creating a flare of sensation that streaked through her. Luca groaned when she tightened around him in response.

He looked deep into her eyes as he shifted his hips. The slight, stretching ache was forgotten in the wake of pleasure when he experimentally rocked against her. His stroke was gentle at first, as he gauged her reaction. Anika wanted more. She could feel the tension thrumming through his body. The last thing she wanted was for him to hold back. Anika didn't want anything to hinder his pleasure. Especially when he was giving her so much. "I want all of you."

The glint in his eyes when she said it hitched her breath. Luca drew back and thrust deeply. The impact knocked the breath from her lungs. He did it again and again, slowly dragging his huge erection past her sensitive flesh, eliciting the most superb sensations with the friction. When he picked up the pace, it was all she could do not to start crying out from the pure decadence of being completely possessed by him.

Luca let loose and set a hard, driving rhythm that quickly had her toes curling again.

Anika cried out his name as her orgasm hit her, tearing through her from the tips of her toes to the top of her head. Luca plunged into her, dropping his head to her shoulder as he groaned his release. She felt every pulse as he came, which only protracted her own pleasure.

He stayed pressed skin to skin with her for a long while. His fast, shallow breaths matching hers. Anika stretched, enjoying the feel of his weight on her. He rolled back, taking her with him.

She was sure the dazed look in his eyes was mirrored in her own.

"Are you okay?"

Better than okay. "I feel... That was wonderful." The words didn't express what she felt.

As she searched for another, he smiled and pressed a gentle kiss to her lips. "It's never been like that for me either."

Truly? Sighing, she smiled.

Luca eased himself out from under her. "I need to take care of..." He looked down. "I'll be right back."

Anika watched him stride into the adjoining bathroom totally comfortable with his nakedness. And why shouldn't he be? The man was amazing to look at and otherwise.

Unsure of what to do, she crawled under the covers, smiling inanely over the fact they hadn't even made it that far. The crisp cool thousand thread count sheets felt wonderful against her heated skin. Her eyelids fluttered shut when she pressed her face against the pillow. She just had amazing sex with Luca Rossi...less than a week after her wedding had fallen through with another man. Anika wasn't sure if she should be pleased or mortified.

Instead of mulling that over, she stuck with the facts. She and Luca had just been intimate and he'd treated her with total respect. Not only that, but the experience had been absolutely amazing.

It occurred to her that he'd never answered the question of which boat was his. "So which boat *was* yours?"

"None of them." His voice drifted from the bathroom just before he stuck his head out. "I don't have one...yet."

For some reason, instead of feeling annoyed at being cheated, the revelation was uproariously funny. Laughing, she threw a pillow at him as he returned to the bed. "You cheated."

Luca deftly caught it and dropped it back on the bed as he slid back in to curl around her. "I won."

She smiled into his chest. "I think you owe me for taking advantage."

His chuckle reverberated through her. "How should I make it up to you?"

"I'm sure you can think of something." Anika wriggled against his hard body. Already she could feel his renewing interest growing against her hip. Again, so soon? Luca curled his hands around her hips and pulled her back against him. "Are you up for round two?"

"I think I could be persuaded." He wouldn't have to try hard either. The liquid ache between her legs grew in anticipation of having him back inside her body.

He laughed softly against the side of her neck. "I'll have to pull out all the stops, then." Luca eased out from behind her to get off the bed and retrieve the cherries and champagne as well as a condom from the drawer in the bedside table.

Luca handed her a glass and slipped back between the sheets, gripping his own in his hand. He took a sip of the champagne and urged her to do the same with a waggle of his brows.

Anika took a cherry and popped it into her mouth, followed closely by a swig of the drink.

Luca kicked off the sheets then snared a cherry by its stem. He dragged the cool berry up her leg in a slow sweep. Conversely, the icy sensation of it on her skin created a trail of heat wherever it touched. He swept it over her lower abdomen, dipping it briefly into her belly button. He dragged it upward around her breast and over the upper curve, off her nipple and into his mouth.

He took her glass from her and nudged her back so she lay flat.

"What are you doing?"

He hushed her with a glance. As if he had all the time in the world, he drained his glass then the rest of hers. Transferring the glasses to one hand, he fished out the strawberries and held them over her mouth. "Open."

She did it without question and he pushed the plump berry between her lips.

"Hold it there."

She watched mesmerized as he dragged the other over her chin and down her body in an achingly slow trek, leaving a cool liquid trail. She closed her eyes when he nudged her legs apart with his knees, leaving her no doubt where the other was going to go.

They snapped open again when he wedged the cold strawberry between her folds. Finally, he picked up the bottle of champagne and dribbled it over her in fizzing drops, most of it pooling in her belly button from the feel of it.

He sat back to appraise his work. "Beautiful."

The combined flavors of champagne and strawberry dripped on her tongue as she continued to watch Luca. He dipped his head to sample one nipple, curling his tongue around it and sucking gently.

Anika arched off the bed, pressing more of her breast into his mouth, seeking the moist heat and pleasure that his touch gave her.

He let it slip from his mouth when she sagged back to the bed, licking a trail to do the same to the other.

She moaned, unable to do much more than that around the fat strawberry. When she tried to hold his head to her breast, Luca took her hands and pinned them above her head in one of his.

"Don't move."

He chuckled when she narrowed her eyes to glare at him. Luca continued his unhurried pace licking up each droplet in turn as he glacially worked his way down her body. He slowly built her arousal, teased and tickled with nothing more than his tongue until she writhed mindlessly seeking more.

Luca sucked the champagne from her belly button with a gleeful slurp. He lifted his head to give her a wicked smile before he hitched her knees over his shoulder.

Anika couldn't stop the moan as he sucked and nibbled the fruit. His breath feathered over her clit. His stubble grazed her delicate inner thigh. The rasp of its delicious counterpoint to the velvet glide of his tongue.

With each delicate bite, she climbed higher. Sparks flared in her vision getting brighter until he sucked the last bit of the berry out with a pop and they exploded as she came against his mouth.

Luca didn't give her a chance to come down before he took half the strawberry from her mouth with a bite and slammed into her with one sure thrust.

She ate what he left as he arched against her, driving himself deep and hitting a deliciously sweet spot. Luca repeated the move when she let out a keening cry in response. Over and over again, he drove the head of his cock into the spot, stealing her breath with sensation it created.

"Come for me. One more time," he growled.

Luca circled her clit with his thumb and it was all she needed to rocket into paradise again. The fluttering grasp of her internal muscles gripping his cock must have pushed him over the edge, because Luca shouted, holding himself as deeply as he could inside her as he came.

Her week was officially looking up.

Chapter Six

"Anika."

She awoke with a start, alone in the expansive bed. Squinting against the bright morning sunshine, Anika stared blearily at her surroundings. The day before came screaming back in a flood of images. Her body ached but still flared to life as she recalled the way Luca had made her feel.

Speaking of Luca, where was he?

"Anika?"

She looked up to see that he'd stuck his head out of the en suite door, accompanied by a plume of steam.

"Care to join me for a bath?"

"I would love to."

"Good."

Luca walked back to the bed and, when she flipped the sheets back, he swept her up into his arms.

"And the man has a romantic streak too, I see."

He chuckled. "I never knew I had it in me."

The bathroom gleamed in the morning light spilling in from the huge, unobstructed windows. The set up was strangely intimate and vaguely exhibitionist at the same time. There was no way anyone could see them bare under the sun with the sparkling ocean and cloudless sky spread out before them.

The marble decorating every inch of the space had been polished to a high shine. Even the massive tub itself had been hewn from the stone. Instead of sitting on the floor like the one in her room, his was sunken into it. A ring of black, smoothed pebbles ran around the edge, disguising the overflow. Luca had arranged at least a dozen frosted, gold-capped bottles from the Totally Five Star line of toiletries along one side.

He sat her on the edge opposite, and Anika eased herself into the perfumed water. A long soak would do wonders for her little aches.

He slipped in behind her. Even though she couldn't be more sated, awareness of his body against hers, wet and hot, wasn't something she could ignore. His long legs rasped hers as she sat in the V of them. Apparently, he was just as affected as she was if the erection growing against her back was anything to go by.

Luca settled in cradling her as though it was something they did every day. "Are you sore?"

It wasn't the water that heated her cheeks. "A little." Was it any wonder? She might not know much about the size of men, but Luca was plenty big enough for her.

"I should have been gentler." He pressed his lips against the side of her neck in apology.

"You were wonderful." Anika couldn't imagine a more perfect first — and second — time.

She lay back on him, enjoying the quiet companionship. That was until she got a splash of water to the face. "What was that for?" she spluttered.

"Just making sure you're still awake."

Anika cupped some water and launched it over her head at him. And before she knew it, they were having a water fight. Even with the size of the tub, it didn't take them long to nearly empty it. She was cold, shivering but smiling from ear to ear.

He got out first, grabbing a towel to throw around her as he lifted her out. Luca wrapped another around his lean hips. Taking her hand, he led her out to the room. Instead of ushering her to the bed as she expected, he opened the balcony doors. Winding his arms around her from behind, he walked them out onto the terrace.

"Luca!" Someone would see them. She tried to dig her heels in but being as big as he was her attempts weren't stopping him.

He pressed her against the balustrade. "Relax. It's not like I'm going to ravish you out here, not that anyone would see if I did."

How could he be so sure? And the not-ravishing-her part set off a twinge of disappointment.

He was right, however. The only way anyone would see them was if they were flying or on the ocean with a telephoto lens. The possibility of that weighed like a lead ball in her gut, but the touch of Luca's hands made her forget about everything except him.

Luca couldn't help but notice the way Anika fit against him. He braced his hands on either side of her as she looked out at the sea, her pert ass notched nicely against his groin. The hard-on he'd been sporting since he'd first seen her still hadn't gone away, even after the night before. He'd lain awake for most of it, aching for her again. It didn't seem right to wake her just to slake his lust so soon after her first sexual experience. It didn't stop him from imagining how he would take her from behind. Or waking her by lashing her clit with his tongue again. Anika had enjoyed everything they'd done so far. She couldn't get angry being roused from sleep that way.

But he had held off. Not just for decency's sake, but because he knew the wait would make the next time even better.

Luca ignored the little siren in the back of his head over the fact that he was planning their next encounters when he meant to forget about her after the weekend.

He made sure she felt his erection against her ass. The decision would be up to her, but she was going to his damnedest to sway things his way. Luca ran a hand up her side stopping just shy of cupping the underside of her breast. "So what should we do today?"

Anika shifted slightly so his thumb and forefinger touched her breast. "I don't know. What else is there to do...here?"

He shifted so his cock fit in the cleft of her ass. "I can think of a few things we haven't tried yet." A great many things.

"I think I'm up for whatever you can think of."

He would make sure of it. But he would have to proceed slowly. The last thing he wanted was to push her too far too fast.

"First I think some breakfast is in order. I'm famished." He was positive he wasn't the only one.

"Food sounds great." She stretched, rubbing herself against him. "I should go back to my room and get dressed, though."

"I think what you have on is perfect." Luca let his eyes rove over her.

She laughed. "Do you?"

"Actually..." He spun her around so she faced him and whipped the towel off her. "Now you're perfect."

Anika gasped as she tried to cover herself. "Luca!"

He dropped his towel as well and all protest died as her gaze raked over him. Luca felt a surge of pride when she forgot everything as she stared at him. Her breath caught, lifting her breasts. Color rose in her cheeks, her chest.

"Not so bad when we're both bare-assed, is it?"

That snapped her out of it. Anika's eyes widened as she grabbed his hand and dragged him inside. Instead of being angry, she shook with laughter. A huge grin lit up her face as she pointed a finger at him. "I can't believe you did that."

He swept her into his arms, enjoying the feel of wriggling, laughing female. The lightness of his heart wasn't a feeling that he was used to. There wasn't a time in recent memory he felt so free. Not before he met Anika.

Luca pushed the thoughts away. Why waste brainpower on useless musings when he had a beautiful, naked woman in his arms?

After picking her up, he wound her legs around his hips and carried her to the bed. Devouring her mouth as he lowered her onto it. He relinquished her for only as long as it took to find a condom and quickly don it. Seconds later, he slid over her again, dragging his skin against hers deliciously and sank into her wet, hot slit. So tight, she fit him exquisitely.

The night before had been for her. In deference to her virginal state, he had taken his time to relax her, prepare her. Now, however, the urge to feel her under him—snug around him—as hard and as fast as he could, was undeniable.

"Luca!"

Anika's excited gasp spurred him on. Pulling back, he thrust back in, fast and deep. Again and again and again. The grip of her pussy around him incredible.

She dropped her head back, her lips parting as she panted. For an instant, Luca feared he had hurt her, but she reared up with a lustful glitter in her eyes. She met his thrusts wantonly, seeking her own pleasure.

Luca's universe narrowed to focus only on the woman under him and the pleasure he derived from her body. He had never experienced anything like it before. Anika was intoxicating. He was addicted to her and, like a drug, he needed more and more. The feel of her against him, her voice as she cried out his name, the intense physical pleasure that he found with her. He couldn't get enough. Couldn't get deep enough. He wanted to leave her trembling, breathless and unable to walk properly for the next few days.

Luca needed to leave her as addicted to him as he was to her.

The thought of Anika wobbling around gap legged because of him made his balls ache even more. Luca wasn't proud of the caveman urge or how quickly he climbed to orgasm. It took all his concentration and self-control to drive Anika over the edge before following her.

Thank God she was so responsive.

Luca was so close—seconds away from exploding—when he felt the telltale fluttering of her muscles around his cock an instant before her eyes closed and she clawed at his shoulders. Her cries and the rhythmic pulse of her orgasm around him dragged him under with her.

He came with a deep groan as he spurted load after load into her until he felt as if he'd emptied his soul into Anika.

Luca rolled off her and stared at the ceiling as he caught his breath. He had never lost control like that before—ever. How could he pounce on her like he did?

But she had enjoyed it every bit as much as he did. A peek at her confirmed it. She looked dazed but there was a sated smile curving her lush mouth.

He loved that they were so compatible.

Loved.

The word blared in his mind and might as well have been a mental bucket of ice water thrown over himself. They'd known each other a day at the most. Love was most definitely not on the table. It was an illogical thought brought on by good sex and nothing more. He liked Anika—there was no question about it. She was a breath of fresh air, beautiful, smart, genuine and fantastic in bed. But there was no love.

There couldn't be.

So why did he feel as though his life had been completely derailed by her?

He didn't like the strange mix of emotions flooding his system. Luca controlled his life, his destiny. It had taken iron will to get where he was and nothing would change who or how he was.

Nothing and no one would take away his command of himself and his life.

Luca shifted to turn to his side, facing away from her to stare at the blurred blue of the ocean in the distance.

The blind stare was interrupted by Anika's beautiful face hovering over his. She looked troubled, serious. He snapped out of his trance immediately. Concern fluttered in his chest.

Luca sat up and cradled her cheek. "What is it? Did I hurt you?"

She shook her head, sending her hair tumbling about her shoulders in ebony waves. "I should go. I have something…things I need to sort out." She refused to meet his gaze.

A dull ached formed in his chest but he refused to beg her to stay. He managed a glib, "That's fine. I have things I need to see to as well."

Anika paled a little. Her reaction twisted something in his gut, which pissed him off even more.

Her voice was weak when she asked, "Will I see you later?"

"Perhaps. We'll see."

She took a deep breath and by the time she exhaled the last of the air from her lungs and repeated the process, the Ice Princess was back. Anika wrapped the sheet around herself then searched the room for her clothes. Finding them one by one, she quickly slipped her dress on and shoved her undergarments and jewelry in her clutch.

Anika barely spared him a glance as she strode down the stairs. He soft ding as the elevator doors parted and the soft whoosh as they closed behind her.

Her feet couldn't move fast enough to get her to her sanctuary. Things between them were going too fast. Too good. It frightened her. Luca had had her on the balcony naked for goodness' sake and she didn't even care. What kind of woman let herself get in that kind of situation? Then, instead of taking him to task, she'd let him climb on top of her again, bringing her to an almost embarrassingly fast orgasm. If he didn't already know he had her wrapped around his little finger, he did now.

But it had been so good. In the afterglow, her mind had wandered. There were more days of them making love wherever and whenever they could. Walks in the moonlight. Dancing under the stars. Fanciful nonsense she hadn't given thought to since she'd read romance novels hidden in the tiny room she shared with Petra at school.

Once she'd wrenched her mind away from them, she noticed Luca's reaction to what they had just shared. She had felt him retreat emotionally before he literally turned away from her.

So she made an excuse to leave. Partially as a test to gauge his reaction. Besides the concern he might have hut her, he didn't seem too bothered. He'd probably had his fill of her.

She cringed at the thought. Tears threatened to fall, but she wouldn't allow it. Anika De Winter didn't cry over men. Not even one as handsome and charming as Luca Rossi.

She managed to make it to her room without anyone seeing her. Although she was sure whoever manned the cameras tucked discreetly in the corners was probably amused.

Fighting the urge to throw up her middle finger at the one down the hall from her room, she unlocked the door and charged inside. Safe in her sanctum, she let herself breathe and wrestled with her thoughts. He'd all but outright rejected her and yet all she wanted to do was to run right back up there, tear off the dress and beg him to take her again.

Disgusted with herself, she dropped her clutch and shoes and headed straight for the bathroom.

With the hot water on full blast, she did her best to scrub him off and beat some sense into herself at the same time.

By the time she got out, Anika felt a bit better. A little self-flagellation via drudgery would help her get the rest of the way to feeling like he usual self.

Wrapped in a fluffy white robe, she ordered breakfast, pulled out her phone and laptop and did what she should have done when she had first arrived. Work.

She sent Petra a text letting her know she was doing okay. Her family got the same message. Anika dove into emails and calls over the small meal. By all accounts, she should have been starving, but she only picked at the scrumptious-looking food. She told herself it was because she was busy with work, but the truth niggled at the back of her mind.

Luca had gotten to her. What was worse, he didn't seem as affected. What had she been thinking? That was the problem. She hadn't been. Or at least not with her head. This was exactly what had spent her life avoiding and less than a day with Luca had ruined it.

What she needed to do now was chalk the whole thing down to experiencing something new. She'd done it. It was great. Time to move on. Only she couldn't get her mind past the vivid images of Luca to focus on the work in front of her.

She was being an idiot. Women had sex all the time and didn't go stupid. Just because Luca had been incredible and the past few days had been a fantasy break from her life didn't mean she should forget about everything else.

It was just sex.

Great sex.

Incredible, even.

That she wanted more of.

Anika slammed the laptop shut.

A walk. That would get rid of some of the pent-up energy. There was plenty to do on her own. The city was nothing if it wasn't a tourists' paradise.

She quickly dressed in a loose, sleeveless black maxi dress, giant sunglasses, and a big floppy sun hat. Besides being cool and covering her from the heat, her ensemble also disguised her nicely. It wasn't like her to hide away from the world, but since when had this trip been about being her usual self? The whole thing had been a diversion from her real life, only now she needed a detour from her diversion as well.

Anika caught a glimpse of the water and she knew the perfect place to go. She quickly stripped, put on a bathing suit, redressed, then stuffed her phone, e-reader, a wallet, a bottle of water from the fridge, sunblock and the room key in the tote she was she glad she'd brought. *Might as well make a day of it.*

Lying on the beach, reading something other than project reports, and soaking up the sun might be exactly what she needed.

And getting away from Luca couldn't hurt either. If out of sight out of mind did the trick then maybe adding distance would help even more.

* * * *

Luca couldn't stand being in his suite any longer. He'd taken breakfast, made calls and stared blindly at his laptop for too long. And none of it made a tiny bit of difference. He couldn't stop thinking about Anika. It was the room. It had to be. He could still smell her and it made his wayward body impossible to control. It didn't help that everything in the room seemed to bring back memories of her — the bed, the bathroom, balcony, even the goddamn floor reminded him of her discarded clothes.

He scrubbed his hands through his hair. He was going to drive himself insane if this kept up.

Cursing, he stuffed his feet into the closest pair of shoes and walked out of the door. He strode through reception, contemplating if he should move rooms. He quickly shoved the thought aside. He wasn't going to let the mere memory of a woman drive him out of there. What he needed was to get her out of his system.

After the way she'd left that morning, it was going to be a hard sell. He wouldn't be surprised if she'd already left. Not that it mattered. If he wanted to find her, there wasn't anything in the world that could stop him.

The thought of her running off without so much as a goodbye irritated him. Panicked him. His self-acclaimed impulse control in tatters, he tramped a path to her room and pounded on the door.

No reply.

He tried again, but when no one but a nosy neighbor opened their door, he had no choice but to stop.

Damn her! She *had* left!

Should he go down to reception? Demand to know if she truly had gone? Luca waved off the thoughts, even as he made his way down to the lobby. Had he no self-respect left? Obviously not where she was concerned.

As he muttered oaths, he walked past the desk and into the glaring sunshine. It did nothing to improve his mood. Glowering at everything in sight, he started walking. Not caring where he went, he set off through the throngs of people, past cars he usually would have taken note of, along the baking-hot sidewalk. Luca was dimly aware of any of it.

He was a mess and it annoyed the shit out of him.

No woman had ever taken over his thoughts as she had. Had been so pervasive. Gotten so deep under his skin. And so fast, she'd flipped his entire world, and all his beliefs, upside down.

Luca didn't like not being in control of his own thoughts or actions. Even less enjoyable was the feeling he'd lost her.

Rubbing the heel of his hand against the hollow feeling in his chest, he walked straight to the water. He let it lap at the toes of his shoes, not caring they were worth more than he cared to remember.

The water had been his siren's call as a child. Even now, he felt freer staring out at the undulating sea. The limpid blue water winked and sparkled, playing with the sunlight. The heat of the sun on his skin was randomly cooled by the salty sea air that alternately rushed and ebbed around him.

Inhaling deeply, he tried to relax his muscles. They refused. The only thing he could think of doing to get them to unwind was impossible without Anika. He wanted her under him again. Preferably tied up and begging him to take her. Or maybe he'd teach her how to ride him. Imagining her pert little breasts bouncing against his lips wreaked havoc on his system. His cock throbbed to life at the mental image. His already taut muscles went rigid. Thinking of her was definitely counterproductive if he was going to get his body to settle down.

Stretching, he forced himself to breathe again. This time, as he slowly inhaled, he caught a different scent mingling with the sea. The delicate aroma had been imprinted on his mind and was unmistakable.

Anika.

It was as though his entire body focused on the single-minded task of zeroing in on her. He turned into the breeze but, of course, it had stopped. He looked up and down the beach, searching for her. The people on the pristine stretch of sand lay spread out, making a visual scan of the area a bit easier, but he couldn't see her anywhere.

He had to be imagining things. Further proof that he was going out of his mind.

Luca turned back to look at the water. He would find her. England wasn't far away and London wasn't too big to search. It would only be a matter of time before she showed up.

Morosely, he stood watching the boats, the people, the water. The sun sank lower and lower, toward the water mirroring his mood.

It was time to get back to reality. As he started walking back up the beach, as he pulled his phone out of his pocket, he saw her.

She hasn't left! His heart bobbed as he approached her.

Anika lay asleep on a sun lounger under an umbrella. In a sedate black one-piece that was tasteful, for sure, but covered way too much of her for his liking.

The sun had barely kissed her skin, thankfully. If she had fallen asleep under the sun, she would have been burned to a crisp. But her pale skin, though it had a new glow to it, hadn't reddened. The hat and sunglasses that would have hidden her from his view lay on the sand, pinned down by her bag.

Unabashedly, he let his gaze wander over her. She looked so peaceful it was almost a shame to wake her. At least that's what he told himself as he stared at her. Anika would have been incensed with the way he now studied her, Luca was sure. So he would look his fill while he could.

His gaze started at her feet, tracing her dainty little toes. He followed her long, lean legs upward to stop momentarily at her breasts before sweeping up to her lovely face.

She shouldn't have been out there alone, especially asleep. Anything could have happened to her. Any lecher off the street could have taken her. A spike of anger laced with fear lanced through him. Had she no sense whatsoever?

Luca wasn't sure if he wanted to kiss her for still being there or throttle her for her carelessness.

Kneeling next to her, he couldn't stop staring at her plump lips and gave into his impulse to remind himself of her taste.

Anika was roused from sleep by a delicious kiss. She enjoyed it for a few moments before realizing it wasn't a dream. That the tongue tangling with hers belonged to Luca, a fact she didn't have to open her eyes to discern. She tasted him. Smelled him. Felt his presence, though the only part of him touching her was his mouth.

His talented, luscious mouth.

She shoved him off before opening her eyes. When her gaze caught his, he looked as aroused as she didn't want to feel. Anika shot up in her seat and shoved him farther backward. "What do you think you're doing?"

The smile he gave her was pure wickedness. "Waking *la bella addormentata*?" He stood, looming over her. "That better question is—have you lost your mind? Falling asleep on a public beach. You could have been kidnapped or assaulted!"

His imperious tone rankled her, even if he was right. It hadn't been her intention to fall asleep there. She had just been so comfortable and relaxed that she couldn't keep her eyes open. "I can do what I want. You have no right to tell me what to do." Incensed, she levered herself off the lounger, grabbed her things and stomped her way back toward the hotel. The peace she'd gained from her day on the sand obliterated by a few words from Luca.

Luca closed his big hand around her arm, holding her fast. "Someone has to when you obviously lack any sense in that beautiful head of yours."

Anika glared at him as she tried to extricate herself from his grasp. His grip was like a vise, although it didn't hurt. She gave up after a few seconds. "It wasn't like I came down here to sleep."

"And yet it happened."

He tugged her close so she could feel the heat emanating from him.

"I have half a mind to spank you for it."

His words should have annoyed her. Who was he to spank her for some imagined slight? But the thought of him bending her over his knee sent a shaft of heat through her that seemed to streak straight to the apex of her thighs. "You wouldn't dare," she gasped, though her lack of breath wasn't entirely due to outrage.

"Wouldn't I?"

He grazed his other hand over the delicate skin of her throat up toward her cheek.

"You should be more careful."

Could he actually be concerned about her welfare? Anika didn't know if it was a hunch she should believe. But he did seem genuinely relieved to see her. She still didn't like being treated like a child. "I will be. You don't need to worry about me."

"But I do." The growling way he said it made her believe it wasn't something he wanted to feel or admit to. "Come. It's getting dark. We should get back to the hotel."

Confusion clouded her mind. She wasn't sure what to think about him. Anika did agree that it was time to return, however. She stepped out of his grasp and resumed her trek back to the hotel, not caring to reply or to check if he followed her. She could hear Luca's footsteps closing in behind her for a few moments before his lengthy strides ate up the distance and he flanked her.

Glad he didn't seem to want to break the silence, Anika hurried along. It was obvious no matter how fast she went, he would be able to keep up since his legs were so much longer than hers. Still, she kept a brisk pace, hoping her silence and her refusal to look at him would give him a big enough hint that she didn't want him around.

Luca simply walked with her. Not touching. Not talking. Anyone who saw them would think they were two strangers who happened to be strolling the same way.

Anika squeezed her eyes closed for a moment. Why did it bother her? She didn't want to talk to him anyway. So why wouldn't he just go away?

Once they were in the lobby, he slowed, grazing her arm with his hand to get her to do the same. "How about we get some dinner?"

"I'm tired. I'll get something in my room." She looked at him levelly. "Later."

"I'll join you."

"Luca—"

He put up his hand. "I'm sorry about the way I spoke to you on the beach."

And that was supposed to make up for it? What about earlier? She'd had a life-altering experience with him and he just brushed it aside. Then again, she hadn't helped things by trying to put some space between them. She just didn't know how to handle the situation. She sighed. "Thanks, but if it's all the same to you, I'd rather be alone."

"I'd rather you weren't." Luca took her hands and pressed his lips against her knuckles. "Let me make it up to you."

She had to admit, a small part of her was charmed. Anika tamped it down. "And how do you think you're going to manage that?"

He winked mischievously at her. "Any way you'd like."

Chapter Seven

She was an idiot. That was the only reason she could think of for letting him follow her back to her room. Lust had made mush of her brain. It was the only explanation. First, she'd fallen into bed with Luca, then she'd passed out on the beach. And now she was in a room containing a bed with him once again. Completely unwise. Perhaps it would be better to go down to dinner.

Anika waved at the couch. "Have a seat while I get changed."

"Changed?" He looked at her questioningly. Anika got the distinct feeling he was imagining her in another outfit — one that showed much more skin.

"You wanted to go to dinner, didn't you?" She didn't wait for his reply and walked straight into the bathroom to take a quick shower and wash the day off her.

She rushed through her routine half expecting him to barge in. When she made it through unscathed, Anika wasn't sure if she was let down or not. The confusion over that alone irked her. Of course, she wasn't disappointed.

She took the other door directly to the bedroom and searched through the clothing she'd brought to find something suitable for dinner. The night was warm enough for her to choose a simple white asymmetrical dress that hung off her right shoulder. It draped loosely, flowing to her knees, making it comfortable with the added bonus of not drawing attention to her figure. She applied her makeup lightly, found a pair of shoes to complement her dress and she was ready to go.

When she returned to the living area, she found that Luca had also changed into dinner attire. No wonder he hadn't bothered her. He hadn't been around. The thought made her feel a little better.

Luca looked wonderful as always in a dark jacket and crisp, white shirt. The open collar invited her fingers to touch and explore. She clenched her hands at her sides to prevent herself from doing so.

Luca's keen eyes caught the movement. "I hope you don't mind. I let myself back in. I didn't want to delay dinner any longer than necessary."

"That's fine." She brushed her hair over her shoulder. "Shall we go?"

"If you're ready."

What was that supposed to mean? She craned her neck to get a glimpse of herself in one of the mirrors by the door.

He curved his arm around her waist as he leaned in close to whisper. "You look fantastic."

His touch frazzled her nerves. Luca was like lightning to her system. The simplest look or touch had the ability to wipe her mind and charge her body. "Thanks."

Luca led the way down to the restaurant, and they were immediately whisked to a private table on the balcony.

"I guess you were up to more than changing while I was in the shower." Anika was enchanted by the view. The soft rushing of the water in the distance, the air perfumed with salt, exotic flowers and the meals of the other diners, all came together deliciously. She swayed gently with the music played from a source unseen, but she knew live instruments when she heard them. Everything about the restaurant was pristine white, even the flowers overflowing from the vases in the corners of the terrace and on the tables. The gleam of the delicately gilded place settings added to the sheen. Even the staff, dressed in black and white, added to the glamour as they glided between the tables in what may as well have been a well-choreographed dance.

Luca smiled as he pulled a chair out for her. "When you said you wanted to come down for dinner, I wanted to make sure that we would be accommodated."

Anika sidestepped him. "Just give me a second. I want to see what the view looks like from here." She walked up to the bannister and peered into the growing darkness. It was breathtaking. Under the light of the moon, the entire scene was magical.

That was until Luca came up behind her and wrapped himself around her. Anika could hear the whispers. He was indecently close and of course, it set tongues wagging. "Luca!"

"Anika, you have to sit." His voice was gruff as he ground out the words. Luca urgently guided her to the seat he had originally taken against the wall.

"What's wrong?"

He glared at every man who dared look in their direction before he snarled at her. "Nothing."

Anika knew something was most definitely wrong but had no idea what. She darted her gaze around to the other tables and saw eyes on them. The men looked at her with barely concealed lust while their dining companions glared daggers at her. Her back stiffened as she looked to Luca for an explanation.

Luca glowered at the table closest to them, challenging the idiot there to keep staring before turning back to Anika. She seemed truly unaware. "Your dress is translucent in the moonlight," he growled.

She gasped and turned her gaze down at herself. The fabric appeared fine now, but when she'd stood at the railing, the moonlight had lit her up like an angel — an angel with a body that made men sit up and beg. Thankfully, he'd got her to sit down before anyone got too good a look. Not that she hadn't already attracted the attention of every red-blooded male in the vicinity for simply walking into the room. With a see-through dress, Anika was a goddess that no man would be able to ignore.

He wanted to throttle every one of them with his bare hands.

"Do you want to go back to your room?" He hoped the answer would be yes.

"How am I supposed to get back to my room without people gawking?"

"It was the moonlight. It shone through the dress and outlined your body. You really think I would have let you walk in here with a see-through dress without stopping you?" He got up, slipped off his jacket and dropped it over her shoulders. "Does that help?"

"A little." She picked up the menu and scanned it nonchalantly, giving him a front row seat of the Ice Princess in action.

Anika was truly stunning.

"Will you stop staring at me?"

His appraisal stopped at her lips. "I wasn't staring."

"I know when people are staring." Her sapphire blue gaze left the menu to meet his. "And you *were* staring."

"Point out one man here that isn't." He shrugged. "We can't help it, we're not blind."

He watched color creep into her cheeks, even though she fought to keep her serene outward appearance. It only made her more attractive.

Luca waved over the waiter and they ordered. He barely knew what he was doing and simply pointed at things on the menu. He was too busy watching Anika. And getting ridiculously turned on watching her drink water of all things. He shifted uselessly in his seat. There was nothing he could do to relieve the pressure in his groin.

One thing came to mind, but he didn't think Anika would appreciate him spreading her over the table and ravishing her. Giving the other diners something to get a real shock over probably wasn't in the cards. The thought made him smile, though.

"What are you smirking about?"

Why sugar-coat it? "I was just imagining having you on the table right here and now and giving them something to really gawk at."

"Luca!" The blush on her cheeks deepened.

"You did ask." He liked the heightened color his words created on her skin. If he couldn't touch her, he could at least do that much. It was proof that he could get to her.

They sat in silence as they waited for the food to arrive, devouring each other with their eyes. No words were needed. Her glances were loaded with everything he needed to know. She wanted him. No matter how cool she appeared or how tart her words, she couldn't hide the hunger in her eyes when she looked at him.

It boosted his pride, knowing that she was powerless to keep it from him.

Luca trailed his finger down her arm, smiling when she jumped from the light touch as if she had come in contact with a live wire. "How long are you staying in Monaco?" He brought his fingers to hers and laced them together. When she didn't pull away, it confirmed his belief that she was interested.

"I plan on staying a few more days. My friend —" Her eyes widened as if she almost let something slip, immediately catching Luca's attention.

Was she here to meet a friend? A male one? Was she planning to bed him? Anger flared, dropping a red haze over his vision. "What friend? Who are you meeting?"

She gasped. "You're hurting me."

He hadn't realized he'd tightened the grip on her hand so let go. What was it about her that had him losing the tight reins he had on his control? Anika had come into his life like a hurricane, leaving his discipline in tatters. "I apologize."

She wriggled her fingers. "No harm done. And no, I wasn't meeting a friend. It's just a long story. I'm here alone. I was planning for it to stay that way…until you came along."

Relief coursed through his blood. "And now that I'm here with you? Would you like me to stay on as well?"

The question seemed to catch her off guard. Anika was afforded time to answer since the waiter chose that moment to arrive with their starters. Black truffle risotto for her and the rockfish soup for himself.

Once the tantalizing appetizers had been laid out before them and the waiter had discreetly disappeared once again, Luca looked at her. "Well?"

"Don't you have things to get back to?"

"No more than you do. I have my phone, a laptop. I can keep apprised of what's going on just fine." He covered her hand with his, drawing her gaze. "So I ask you again. Do you want me to stay here with you?"

"Yes."

Anika said the word without thinking. If she had thought about it, she probably would have replied in a completely different way. In a manner that would have turned her expectation of spending her vacation alone a reality.

More time with Luca was enticing. Especially when she imagined that time would require varying degrees of nakedness.

That definitely appealed to Anika. She just didn't want things going too far. It would be too easy to get in over her head with a man like Luca. "We should set some ground rules, I think."

"Haven't we already?" Despite his words, he nodded. "I guess we could elaborate."

"Right." She licked her lips before she took a forkful of her meal and tried to put her thoughts into words. She'd never been in a similar situation before, so she wasn't quite sure how things would work. "I still believe that this…whatever *this* is…is best kept to right here and now."

Luca agreed with another nod. "I've found a few rules work best."

Why wasn't she surprised that he had rules for this type of occasion? Interested, she leaned in. "And they would be?"

"Like you said, there is only the here and now. Love isn't on the table. Pleasure is paramount. And when the word 'goodbye' is said, it's forever. Simple."

That pretty much covered everything she was thinking. There really wasn't anything else to add. It was wonderful that he was as pragmatic as she was. There was no talk of 'what-ifs' or dithering about what they were to embark on. Unlike Joshua and his constant concerns of what would happen in the future. He always found something to ask. To worry about. What if they found someone they truly loved? What if they found themselves incompatible?

It was exhausting.

By comparison, Luca was a breath of fresh air. In fact, he was the most invigorating, interesting thing to happen to her in far too long.

She just had to be careful not to lose *her* head. Anika was sure that with Luca it was a dangerous possibility. Hadn't she already dropped her guard around him? He had seen and done more to her than anyone else in the past. And she was willing to let him do more. In fact, she wanted him to.

He tapped her hand. "So? Do you agree?"

Anika nodded slowly. "I do."

"Excellent." He took a spoonful of his soup and sighed happily.

He genuinely looked pleased. Excitement put a tremble in her hands as she tried to eat. Not that she could taste anything. Luca caught her gaze and gave her a gentle smile. As if to say relax. How could she?

"Would you like a taste of the soup?" Luca held out his spoon for her to try a bit.

She stared at his elegant fingers for a moment, remembering what they were capable of. The memories were enough for her to forget propriety and she took the spoon into her mouth.

She heard the catch of his breath when she did and realized she had the same effect on him as he had on her. Anika pulled back slowly, letting the spoon slip out of her mouth. She smiled at him innocently when he almost dropped it. "It's delicious."

In the spirit of reciprocation, she fed him a little of her risotto, enjoying the way his lips closed over the fork. The way he licked his lips and chewed. He made the simple act of eating a sensuous one.

It didn't take long for them to finish the appetizers, and by the time the entrées arrived, Anika squirmed in her seat. She noted that Luca had adjusted himself a few times as well, though his outward appearance didn't show any discomfort.

The chef was on a truffle kick, it seemed. Anika inhaled the complex aroma of her plate—steamed shrimp, fennel with mandarin topped with a truffle vinaigrette—before looking over to see what Luca's plate offered. He had the beef medallion with carrot rosettes and truffles. Both looked incredible.

She speared a shrimp and held it out for him. "These look succulent. Want a bite?"

He came in for a bite, but she held it just out of his reach. Luca inched closer with a mischievous smile, playing along with her game. Anika brought him close enough to press her lips against his. Licking the seam of his lips to gain access, she nibbled his bottom lip when he opened up instead of invading his mouth.

Luca chuckled as he drew back in his seat. "Not half as succulent as your lips, I think."

"You decide." She fed him the shrimp before going for one of her own. Anika took a bite and rolled her eyes back in delight. "It's incredible."

He had frozen in his seat, observing her, rapt.

"What?"

"There is only one other place I've seen you make that face." Luca's smile turned wicked. "I find it difficult to accept that food can give you the same face that I do. I must do better next time."

Her jaw went slack and it took her moment to remember how to swallow. Better? He could do better? She crossed her legs against the ache growing between them.

He delicately wiped his mouth, dropped the napkin on the table and stood. "Come."

Anika was all too eager to follow his lead. She tugged his jacket close and stood. He wrapped an arm around her and they swiftly exited the restaurant.

His quick pace was the only thing giving away his excitement. Anika would have broken into a sprint if she could, but building the anticipation appealed to her. Not that it could build much more. As it was, her legs were made of jelly.

Her suite was closer than the penthouse, so when he reached for the buttons in the elevator, she beat him to it and hit the one for her floor.

Luca pushed her against the wall. He shoved his jacket from her shoulder, dropping his lips to the bare skin beneath. He nipped her gently as he dragged his mouth up her neck to her lips.

She hiked a leg around his lean hip, seeking only one thing — contact.

His kiss was hot, punishing, persuading. As if he needed to cajole her into his bed. She did, however, appreciate the effort. Melting into his arms, she molded herself against him.

The doors parted with a quiet swish. Luca grabbed her hand and tugged her along behind him. Anika had the key card out and ready by the time they reached her door. With a swipe and a kick, they were inside.

Luca deftly shoved the jacket off her shoulders before going to work on her dress. His nimble fingers made short work of the fastenings. Her dress quickly joined the jacket on the floor.

Hating that she was the only one naked, Anika tore open his shirt, needing him bare as quickly as possible. Pressing her palms against the hot, taut skin of his chest, she dug her nails into his hard pecs.

The effect was immediate. Luca picked her up and wrapped her legs around his waist as he ravaged her mouth.

Anika hadn't been aware they'd moved until her back hit the icy wall. The sensation of being pinned between it and Luca's solid body made her smile against his lips.

Luca grinned back before invading her mouth with his tongue and kissing the breath from her lungs. He shifted, replacing the press of his erection against her with his hand. Cupping her mound, he rocked his hand against her. Anika keened at the pleasure streaking through her. And just when she couldn't think it could get any better, the he slipped two blunt tipped fingers inside her.

Her head fell back against the wall as he ground himself against her, crooking his fingers. The pleasure spiraled higher, coiling her body tighter and tighter. He kept her there for a moment—just hovering a hair from bliss—before she exploded, his name a moan torn from her lungs.

Biting her lip, Luca walked into the bedroom, adjusting her in his arms as he went. But instead of placing her on the bed, he turned so that he sat on it and she lay in his lap. His dark brown eyes narrowed speculatively. "I believe I still owe you a spanking."

Anika didn't get a chance to reply before he flipped her over on his lap. She tried half-heartedly to wriggle from his grip, but he held her in place. "Luca!"

"Hush." The biting kiss on the back of her neck stopped her struggling. "If I do anything you don't want, stop me."

She didn't get a chance to register the soft tone of his voice.

The first strike stung, but sent shock waves through her. They ricocheted around her body to pool back at the apex of her thighs. On the second his fingers strayed lower, striking her still ultra-sensitized clit. Moaning from the glorious mix of sensations, Anika ground herself into his lap and subsequently his rock-hard erection. Her nipples brushed over the soft cover of the bed, zapping more electricity into her veins on the next slap.

It wasn't punishment. It was foreplay.

She should have been humiliated. Shamed. Her ass was in the air, getting spanked like it belonged to a naughty child, and Anika had never been more turned on in her life. Something she kept thinking, but Luca always found a way to surpass himself.

By the end of their time together, she would be a quivering mass of goo.

She couldn't wait to see what he did to her next.

Luca smoothed his hand over her pink skin, admiring the rosy contrast to the rest of her pale skin. As he soothed her, he let his hand wander lower to find Anika was wet. He could see the moisture between her thighs, smell her delicate scent in the air. It made his mouth water.

The punishment wasn't intended to hurt. From the looks of it, she enjoyed it more than he did. Anika writhed in his lap, taking pleasure his ministrations, and it only made him grow harder—painfully so.

Anika continued to squirm against him. Not out of discomfort, but because she wanted more sensation. More contact.

And he would give it to her.

It pleased him that she was so responsive to him, so open to new experiences. That she relished his ministrations was a delightful surprise—a most welcome one.

Luca knew how to read people, and someone as uptight and tightly leashed as Anika craved release. He could imagine her life was rigid, filled with rules and pomp. She needed someone to give her a choice. Someone to show her she could break those boundaries. He might have been domineering, but she ultimately decided what she would or wouldn't do. They both knew it. Luckily, for them both, it was his pleasure to give her what she wanted. Her gratification would ultimately lead to his own.

He gently flipped her over and returned his mouth to hers to taste the unique flavor of her lips. Luca couldn't get enough of her. When he'd thought she'd left, he'd actually feared he would never see her again. The thought that she would walk out without a backward glance had hurt. The relief that had flooded through him when he saw her again was bone melting. Of course, he had to ruin it by scolding her. But he had every reason to. Didn't she know how dangerous it was out there?

He shoved aside the unsettling feelings. The ones he needed to concentrate on right now were Anika's and wiping away thoughts of anything or anyone else from her mind.

Or his.

Luca wound her legs around his waist and flipped her under him so he could freely explore her luscious body. Unlike a lot of women in society that he'd encountered, Anika hadn't had the desire to augment her body in any way. He liked that she was comfortable in her own skin. Her breasts were small, something other men might have scoffed at, but Luca preferred natural to a handful of silicone.

The same went for her face. She didn't have the overly puffed lips or stretched face of someone who'd had surgery — surgery which in his opinion only made matters worse rather than better. Anika's natural beauty and innate confidence were an incredible turn-on. Together with everything else, he had learned about her, she was quickly becoming the woman all others would have to measure up to.

Hungrily, he ravaged her mouth as he explored her with his hands. He couldn't help the growl of satisfaction when she did the same, urgently seeking the buttons on his shirt to tear them open so she could touch his hot skin beneath. Luca ground his cock against her, making her mewl and arch against him, seeking more.

Luca sat back on his knees. Anika watched him, her eyes half lidded with passion, her cheeks stained pink, her legs held apart by his knees, so he could see all of her. He quickly shucked his shirt, tossing it aside. After undoing his trousers, he shoved them down his thighs. He swiftly retrieved a condom, donned it and came down to her again. A quick adjustment of himself and he thrust home into her tight, welcoming heat. Luca paused for a moment, deep inside her, just savoring the sensation of her snug and searing hot around him.

Anika rolled her hips, a move that surprised him and roused him further. She was a wanton little thing and though she was inexperienced, she knew what she wanted and was determined to get it.

He slid one hand up her arms to pin her wrists over her head. The other, he skimmed slowly down her side to her hip and held her in place as he thrust deeply, deliberately. "We'll do things my way, *tesoro.*"

His way wasn't good enough. She wanted him wild and uninhibited like the last time they'd been together. After the spanking, she assumed that he would be rough and it was what she wanted—needed. Gentle and slow could wait for another time.

Anika writhed against him. Digging her nails into his scalp, she hauled him closer, biting his bottom lip hard enough to make him growl in response.

His eyes were narrowed and dark when he pulled back to look at her. He slowed his strokes even more so that he dragged torturously inside her. "Am I displeasing you, *cara?* Am I doing something wrong?" The smile he gave her told her he knew exactly what he was doing and that it was far from amiss.

Nothing about what he did was wrong, but she wanted more. Faster. Harder. Now. "Luca, please."

"Please what?" He shifted and changed his movement into a more circular grind of his hips.

Anika clawed at his back as pleasure streaked through her. "I need you..." She arched against him, trying to get him to understand what she craved.

He nibbled the skin under her ear. "If you tell me, you know I will do everything in my power to give it to you."

Somehow, she knew he meant beyond sex. The knowledge curled her toes. "I need you to make me come. I want you deeper. Harder. Make me scream."

Impossibly, Luca's eyes darkened even more. He plunged himself into her, his rhythm setting a pace that rapidly sent Anika spiraling toward a shattering orgasm. As her breaths came harder to catch and started to come in shrieks, Luca kissed her, taking the cries into himself.

Moments later, he thrust hard, pushing himself inside her as far as he could, coming with a shout.

Anika lay floating blissfully in the afterglow as they both tried to catch their breath.

Luca eventually summoned the strength to move. He slid to the side, keeping their bodies in contact. Running his hands over her as if he couldn't help himself, he sighed.

"What?"

"I can't seem to get enough of you."

He wasn't the only one feeling that way. Anika studied him for a long moment. He certainly didn't look happy about his revelation. From the set of his eyebrows, she would have thought he was puzzled. "Is that a bad thing?"

Luca dragged her over so she ended up sprawled over him. There was no way she couldn't tell that he was well on his way to being ready for round two. "Not at all."

She rubbed herself on his hardening shaft, enjoying the way she made him groan. Anika marveled over the power that she had over him. He knew how to make her respond to him, that much was clear. But to have that same command of Luca was wondrous.

He sat her back on his thighs and handed her a condom this time. "Care to do the honors?"

Pinching the little packet between her thumb and forefinger, she looked down at him. It wasn't brain surgery, but it intimidated her a little. She hated not knowing what she was doing.

Luca smiled and gently showed her what to do, disposing of the old one at the same time. It was the first real look she'd had of him—all of him. He was magnificently built and reminded her of the men in portrayed in ancient statues only Luca was a bit bigger, especially in the lower regions. His erection throbbed, big and hard, under her gaze. It was amazing to know *that* fit inside her so well.

And that she wanted it there again.

Luca patiently let her look her fill, watching her right back without any judgment. He seemed perfectly content letting her take her time learning his every line and contour. She had been so sure of what men would be like—what *he* would be like—that the reality of the situation was so much better.

He wasn't greedy. He cared about more than just getting his satisfaction. Her pleasure was as much of a concern for him as his own. Luca was the perfect lover, in her opinion. Not that she had any to compare him to. But it was obvious he'd had plenty of practice to hone his skill—a discomforting thought.

Still, she had him to herself for the next few days. Anika would make the most of it. If anything she'd learn a trick or two from the master.

"What are you thinking?"

His deep voice drew her out of her reverie. "Just reminding myself to make the most of the time we have."

A smile slowly spread over his features. "I couldn't agree more." Luca carefully lifted her off him and pushed her toward the head of the bed. "Why don't we try something different this time around?"

If it made her feel as good as the other things they'd done so far, she was all for it. Anika let him position her on the bed — on her knees, hands on the headboard, facing away from him. She looked over her shoulder at him, "Luca..."

"Not a word. Stare at the wall and no matter what I do, don't look back or let go."

His words frightened her a little. She refused to turn away. "I'm not sure..."

He kissed her gently, caressing her cheek as he did. "I won't do anything to hurt you. If you don't like it, just say the word." Luca nipped her bottom lip. "But I can guarantee you will enjoy it."

Curious, she nodded and assumed the position he'd asked for. Luca pulled her hips back, stroking the curve of her ass for a deliciously long minute. Each time his touch grew lighter until she was so heightened, so anxious for his touch that a whisper of it on her skin became a lick of fire.

Then there was nothing.

She didn't hear him moving. She could barely hear his breath so she knew he was still there, but he didn't touch her.

Anika stayed rigid, keeping her eyes riveted to her hands on the headboard. She clenched and unclenched her fingers as she waited for something — anything — to happen.

Then she felt it, his warm breath on the small of her back just an instant before the searing brush of his lips. And just as quickly as she felt it, it was gone again. The next touch came just below her shoulder. A glide of his fingers, barely making contact on the side of her breast as they passed on their way to her waist.

Anika could scarcely breathe. The strokes came randomly in places that she never would have regarded as erogenous zones. But every part of her he touched became one. A breath on the back of her thighs. His fingers dragging along her calves. And when he pressed a kiss on her ankle, the world tilted on its axis.

Panting, she tightened her grip on the headboard. Pressing her thighs together, she tried to relieve the ache throbbing between them. Her attempt earned her a sharp smack on the ass

"Did I say you could move?" Luca growled.

She was wound so tightly that his voice coupled with the stinging pain nearly set her off. She bit her lip and shifted again—earning her another smack. So close…

He moved closer then, gripping her from behind, giving her much needed contact as he huskily whispered into her ear. "You don't think I know what you're trying to do?" He ground himself against her nearly bringing her to orgasm but stopped just as she started to tremble.

Gasping, she turned to look at him. "Luca, please!"

The wry smile he gave her froze her lungs. Had she ruined it? He only let her fret a moment before he grabbed her hips, thrusting into her fully with one long, hard stroke. Luca didn't give her a chance to adjust to him before he set a pounding rhythm. Not that it mattered, Anika shattered after the first two thrusts, crying out her climax.

His pace never slowed and succeeded in drawing out her orgasm and building it into another, more powerful one that left her limp and replete.

Luca finally reached his peak and slammed into her one last time before he came with a shuddering groan.

He slowly pulled out of her, then helped her into the cool sheets before getting in them himself. Kissing her soundly, he smiled at her. "So was I right? You enjoyed that?"

He knew she did. How could he not? Anika couldn't be bothered to spar with him verbally. She simply nodded and snuggled against him.

Chuckling, Luca wrapped his arms around her. "Just wait until you see what I've got in mind next."

Chapter Eight

Luca left early the next morning, but not before waking her with a kiss and making her promise to join him in his suite for breakfast.

Anika was a little glad for the reprieve. Her muscles ached from the night before. Luca was probably way ahead of her on that. She wondered what he had in mind next. Her dreams were a riot of images and sensations of what they had done and what they could do in the coming days. He wasn't the only one with ideas in mind.

She headed for the bathroom and filled the tub with warm water and a drop or two of whatever was in the bottles left for her to enjoy by the hotel staff. She quickly adjusted the mix to suit her tastes and slipped into the fragrant water. She dunked her head and when she re-emerged, she sighed happily. It was exactly what she needed to soothe her weary body.

A trip to the hotel spa would be in order if she hadn't already had plans with Luca. Somehow, she didn't think that a day of getting pampered and massaged was his idea of fun. Maybe once she got back to London she'd find the time.

She snorted to herself at the thought. Even if she found the time, it would be hard to get to a spa without someone noticing and taking pictures. Anika resigned herself to visit Monaco again. Though she doubted she could without the memories of Luca plaguing her every step.

He had made what started out as an escape into something that she would never forget—for all the right reasons.

Before she got morose thinking about how her life would be without Luca in it, she picked up her phone and checked her email and texts. There were fewer ones from her family. It seemed they had gotten over her disappearance, at least for the meantime. The majority was from work, just progress updates and the like. Mundane minutiae she'd rather put off for later. She scrolled through and answered the most important and time sensitive ones.

Dropping her phone on the floor, she slid down so all was submerged but her head. She lay back against the side and just soaked. It was a rare occurrence. Her usual bathing routine involved a quick shower and spritz of moisturizing mist, if she remembered, as she dashed to work, a meeting, an appearance, or a social function. She couldn't remember the last time she had a long, hot bath before arriving in Monaco. When she usually got in by the end of the day, she was too tired and would just have a quick shower before tumbling into bed.

Another thing she would have to remedy.

It was funny how a few days without a routine had made her rethink hers. Yet, she knew nothing would have changed if it hadn't been for Luca.

Anika stayed in the tub for a little while longer before curiosity got the better of her. She dressed in a simple sundress. Since she had the distinct impression she wouldn't be wearing it for long, she didn't put much thought into it, her make up or her hair. Anika did spend an inordinate amount of time fretting over her lingerie, however. She needed to make a stop at a boutique to buy something new. While she liked having fine underwear, the possibility of someone else seeing it changed matters.

She chuckled. Not once before this trip had she considered what anyone thought of her underwear. Luca didn't seem to have any complaints, but it didn't mean she couldn't keep him on his toes.

Anika made her way up to the penthouse using the extra key card he'd given her. It took mere minutes to arrive in the living area of his suite.

He was nowhere in sight, though she could see into the dining area and saw the sumptuous meal already waiting. "Luca?"

He stuck his head out of the office. "I'm just finishing up some calls. Don't feel that you have to wait for me to start."

Nodding, Anika wandered toward the table and looked at what was offered. From the sheer volume and variety, she had to assume that he'd ordered everything on the menu at least once. There was no way they could eat it all.

Had he invited others to join them for breakfast? If he had, she couldn't very well just start eating. Anika would wait until he got off the phone for verification. Meanwhile, she wandered through the space. The last time she'd been there, Anika hadn't had the chance to explore.

In the light of day, the penthouse looked even better than she remembered. The flowers had been changed out. Instead of the pale assortment of white flowers, the staff had opted for a vibrant mix of reds, giving the arrangements a fiery flash. The cushions on the sofa as well had been changed to match. Did they do this every day? It wouldn't surprise her in a principality so known for its ostentatious flare.

It was perfect.

The doors to the verandah had been opened, and Anika was drawn to the sun-drenched balcony. Would she ever get sick of the view?

"Not hungry?" Luca's voice came from behind her.

She turned to smile. He'd taken a shower that had left his hair still damp. The stubble that had darkened his chin was gone. His rumpled clothing from the night before had been replaced by a crisp white button-down shirt and black trousers. Luca looked primed and ready for anything. "I thought I'd take another little look around."

"By all means." He waved her through. "Anything in particular you wanted to see?"

"No, I was just curious to see what Totally Five Star had to offer its most prestigious guests."

Luca chuckled. "I can't say that I should be ranked with all them. I just happened to manage to get in at the right time."

"So you're just lucky."

His smile grew. "More than you'll ever know."

The statement puzzled her, but she wasn't given the chance to ponder over it. Luca ushered her to the table and sat her down. "What can I get you?"

Anika let her gaze wander over the spread until it lit on something that caught her interest. "Orange juice and a couple of crepes."

Kait Gamble

He deftly served up what she asked for before going for his own. Luca poured himself a coffee, without adding anything to it, and settled down for a small mountain of pancakes drenched in syrup.

Anika's eyes were wide as she watched him devour it bite by bite. "Hungry?"

"Famished." He snatched up a slice of bacon with his fingers and bit into it with a grin. "Aren't you?"

She nodded as she took her first bite. "I thought you might have invited some guests to join us since there was so much food."

His eyebrows lowered together. "Why would I do that?"

Anika shrugged. "I don't know. It was just a possibility that came to mind after I saw the table."

"I'm not interested in spending time with anyone else," he said it nonchalantly as he looked at her. "Are you?"

She hadn't even entertained the thought. "No."

He sat back with his coffee in his hand "I wasn't sure what you would prefer so I thought I'd get a little of everything."

Anika looked archly at the laden table. "A little?"

"I didn't want you to be disappointed." He sipped the coffee before giving her a wicked smile. "Besides, I had an idea…"

Anika let her gaze follow his down to the table, at the fruit, the syrup. Her eyes widened as they met his. "Surely you don't mean to use the food…"

"Why not? It's not like we haven't done it before. Do you have any allergies?" Luca asked with a sardonic tilt to his mouth

For some reason, the question amused her so much she burst into laughter. Luca calmly watched her while she giggled. When it became clear she wasn't about to stop any time soon, he steadily reached over the table, scooped up some cream from the Belgian waffles and flicked the glob onto the front of her dress.

That did the trick.

"What on earth did you do that for?" Anika tugged the loose fabric off her skin as she tried to fish it out. It was too late. The froth had already melted into her clothing. What hadn't turned liquid quickly joined the rest when she touched it.

Luca grinned at her roguishly. "I guess you'll just have to take the dress off."

If that's how he wanted to play…

Anika grabbed the decanter of syrup and stood up.

"Don't."

"Don't what?" She stepped around the table toward him with an innocent smile on her face. "I just thought your pancakes could use a little more syrup."

"Anika…" Luca shoved his chair back just as she tipped it over his chest.

She watched the golden liquid dribble down over his neck and into the open collar of his shirt. "I guess you'll have to take that off too."

He snared her with a lightning-quick grab, twisting her around so she was pinned between him and the table.

Anika grinned up at him before she lowered her head and lapped the syrup clinging to his neck and followed it down over his collarbone with her tongue.

"*Sirena*," he muttered. His hand flexed and released in her hair as if he didn't know whether to pull her back or hold her to him. "You are a siren."

Anika liked that he was putty in her hands. She pushed button after button through the little holes, taking her time, moving down him as slowly as the syrup slid over his skin. She pressed her hands against his hot, taut flesh, loving the feel of the muscle bunching and shifting beneath. The unyielding muscle was a ceaseless source of wonder. Anika didn't think she would ever grow tired of exploring the angles that made up Luca Rossi.

Luca reached behind her and retrieved a strawberry dipped in whipped cream. He held it just out of the reach, teasing her. Before letting her have a bite, he dragged it over her lips, painting them with frothy emulsion. He pushed it into her mouth as he brought his crashing down for a kiss.

The tart sweetness of the berry burst over her tongue mingled with the silky smooth cream and the taste of Luca. A dizzyingly marvelous concoction when coupled with the press of his body against hers.

Luca ravaged her mouth until she relied almost entirely on the table to stay standing. Clinging to him, she held herself against him, wanting to feel more of him — to become one with him.

Anika pushed his shoulders, changing places with him.

Luca gave her an appreciative smile. She had some strength to her. "What are you up to?"

Anika didn't answer him but the wicked smile she gave him piqued his interest. She had been content thus far with letting him take the lead. He wanted to see what she was capable of.

She didn't meet his gaze. Instead, she concentrated on him. His shirt. His chest. She drew his hands to his sides, curling his fingers around the edge of the table, obviously wanting him to keep his hands there. She then deliberately pushed the offending garment off his shoulders and dragged it off to drop it in a heap on the floor. Anika's feather-light touch, her soft skin against his, stoked the fire further.

Then she raked her nails over his abs.

Luca had to grit his teeth to stop from releasing the table to grab her, caress her, bend her over the table and take her. However, he was proud of his control and for the moment, he still had rein over it. Fraying as it was, he willed himself to let her explore.

It was intoxicating watching her as she discovered what he liked, what she liked. Learning the power of her own body.

He was enthralled.

Anika followed the trail of syrup that had been hidden under his shirt, dragging her tongue over his chest and down his abs, flicking it over his muscles.

When she dipped her tongue into his belly button to retrieve the syrup that had pooled there, Luca's jaw dropped. The sensation of her tongue flicking the little hollow was nothing. However, when she gently dropped to her knees, her hands went to the waistband of his trousers.

He leaned back to watch as she unfastened them and pushed them and his underwear down his thighs. What she did next put a smile on his face.

Anika picked up the syrup once more and drizzled it over the head of his cock, letting it dribble over him until he glistened.

She caught his glance and, licking her lips, she took him into her mouth. The heat of her mouth contrasted with the cooler syrup. He gave into his impulse to release the table and tangle his hand in her hair, holding her in place as he fought not to lose control completely.

Her tongue swirled over him as she bobbed her head. He took her hand from its place on his thigh and wrapped it around the base of him, showing her how to stroke him. She easily learned what she needed to do to make him weak in the knees.

"Anika... I'm close." He wanted to give her the choice of whether or not she wanted to see it through to completion. When she looked up at him with her big blue eyes and smiled around his cock, it tipped him over the edge.

Her eyes widened for a second and for an instant he was afraid she was going to back away, but he felt her swallow around him, lick him, taking everything he gave. Luca was in heaven.

He returned his hands to grip the table to keep himself upright.

When she finally let him go, he couldn't find the words, or the breath, to say a thing. He could only look at her in wonder.

"So, did I do well?"

"You really have to ask?" Luca dropped to the floor next to her, boneless and sated. "I don't think I can move."

She laughed. It sounded wonderful and brought a weary smile to his face.

"That wasn't quite how I expected things to go, but I can't say I'm disappointed." He wiped the syrup from her nose. She was incredible. Luca was completely charmed by her innocence. Or at least by how it was being slowly erased and replaced by a seductress. "How about a shower?"

Without waiting for her reply, he stood, letting his trousers drop. Luca kicked them aside before he started walking in the direction of the bathroom, knowing she would follow.

In one of the mirrors, he saw Anika just stared at his naked body slack-jawed for a second before she stood as well and followed. He heard her footsteps catch up to him. Luca led the way and went straight for the huge glass-enclosed shower, turning it on full blast. With a grin, he dragged her in with him to stand under the fall of water. She squealed with laughter as the massive rainfall showerhead drenched them quickly.

Anika looked up at him. "You look happier."

"Do I? He knew he felt lighter, freer. But he'd thought he had better control over his outward expression of his emotions.

"When we first met, you looked so dour. Like the weight of the world rested on your shoulders."

"And now?"

"Well, you're smiling. The set of your eyebrows have smoothed. You just seem happier. Relaxed."

Luca ran his hands over her slick skin. "Perhaps it has something to do with the company I've been keeping."

That made her smile. The thing was, it was the truth. None of it was lip service. Nothing he'd ever said to her had been. They didn't need to be coy.

Definitely a refreshing change from the cloying, game-playing women he'd been mired with for years. If there was a perfect woman out there for him, Anika was pretty damned close to being her.

He scooped her up, cupping her bottom and holding her close, but instead of pressing her against the cold wall, he turned so he took the chill. Luca slid down so she sat straddling him on her knees. "I think one good turn deserves another, don't you think?"

Her pupils dilated until they ate the blue of her eyes. Nodding, she eagerly settled back to give him whatever he wanted.

Luca closed his hands around her breasts first, enjoying the way the water beaded and ran over them. Luca closed his lips around one puckered nipple before sucking it deep into his mouth. Anika keened and arched her back, allowing him better access. Her thighs tightened around him as she rocked her hips against him.

Luca stilled her with his hands on her ass. Holding her tightly, he rolled her so she lay sprawled under him with her face out of the fall of the water.

The rest of her, however…

He sat back and let the shower spray her. On her sensitized skin, it would be exquisite torture. From her reaction, he guessed right. Anika squealed when the water hit her, tried to cover herself, but Luca shook his head. She obeyed and forced her arms to stay on the floor. She wriggled under the barrage of drops, clawing her nails into the marble floor.

She never looked more beautiful.

Luca kissed a path over her abdomen, downward. He hitched her legs over his shoulders and gave her a grin before dropping his head between her thighs.

Anika groaned under the swirl of his tongue. When he sucked her clit, she curled her legs tight around him, holding him close. He took it as a good sign. Smiling, he added two fingers, sliding them into her with a sure stroke, then he crooked them, pumping them slowly.

Anika clamped her thighs around his head and shoulders as he worked his fingers in and out of her in tandem with the lashing of his tongue. When her legs started to tremble and her voice rose several octaves, he sucked her little bud between his lips and sent her screaming over the edge.

She could have drowned right there on the floor of the shower and she wouldn't have cared. The waves of bliss finally ebbed, leaving her dazed, languid and staring up at him in wonder.

"So how did I do?"

He was mocking her and she knew it. Anika just couldn't find the energy to take the bait.

"Food. I need food."

"Then, by all means, let me feed you." Luca chuckled and held out a hand to her.

She took it and let him help her to her feet. While she turned off the water, he quickly found towels and handed one to her. He tucked the other around his hips and led the way back to the table.

They enjoyed a leisurely breakfast. After their interlude in the shower, the sexual tension between them had dulled, replacing it with a wonderful euphoria. What would it be like to do this all the time? Whenever they liked? All over the world? It didn't even have to involve travel. She would enjoy time with him wherever they were. It didn't matter what they were doing.

Anika nearly choked on her waffle when she realized what she was thinking. This was ending in a matter of days. She had to remember that.

"Is something wrong?"

Shaking her head, she took a sip of her coffee. "What are we going to do today?"

"I thought we'd explore the Japanese Gardens. Or if that doesn't interest you, there are several museums we could check out."

"Sounds like a plan." She fingered her limp hair and eyed the pile of clothes on the floor. "I'll have to get re-dressed. But it shouldn't take me long."

He shrugged. "No rush." Luca raked her with his gaze. "In fact, I think we can check them out later."

She laughingly let him throw her over his shoulder and carry her to the bedroom.

Anika bounced off the bed when he dropped her onto it. Jokingly, she tried to crawl over the expanse of bed away from him. Luca easily hooked an arm around her waist and pulled her back toward him.

He nipped the back of her neck playfully. "Trying to get away from me, are you?"

Before she could reply, he wriggled his fingers over her ribcage tickling her mercilessly.

Anika squealed, kicking and squirming to get out of reach, but the more she wriggled against him, the more aroused she became. She wasn't the only one. Anika felt the press of his erection against her long before he stopped the torture.

"Stay where you are. Don't move," he commanded.

The telling bounce of the bed let her know he had climbed off. She craned her neck to see what he was up to and spotted him retrieving and putting on a new condom. She turned away just as he looked in her direction.

"What did I say?" Luca slipped into the bed behind her and spooned himself around her.

Her mind went blank the instant his body came into contact with hers. The heat from him, the feel of his hard-on against her, the scent of him. Luca filled her senses until there was nothing else.

He nudged her leg up with his knee and slipped the head of his erection just inside her. When Anika tried to slide back, he held her hips tight.

Her inner muscles clenched unsatisfyingly, needing more than just the broad head. She needed all of him deep inside her.

Luca nibbled her earlobe. "Tell me what you want."

She tried to edge back again, but he was too strong for her. "You, Luca. I need you."

He pulled her back against him, roughly seating his cock fully in one thrust. The feel of him knocked the breath from her lungs.

Luca set a gentle pace, rocking in and out of her leisurely as he held her in place. Anika loved it, but it wasn't enough. Try as she might, there was nothing she could do to change the pace. Not held as she was.

His breath was hot on her neck as he groaned, "Something wrong?"

She clawed at his thigh, trying to spur him into thrusting harder. "Luca, please."

He continued his infuriatingly slow pace, the deep yet gentle thrusts. "Please what, *cara*? Tell me what it is you want."

"I want you to fuck me, Luca."

His chuckle turned into a groan as he increased the intensity of his thrusts. Not only that but he curled one arm under her leg, keeping it in the air while he toyed with her clit. The light circles combined with the driving thrust of his thick cock easily brought Anika to orgasm.

Luca's rhythm faltered as he too joined her with a succession of rapid thrusts and a rumbling groan as he pulsed inside her.

Chest heaving, he fell back, taking her with him. He quickly took care of the condom before wrapping his arms around her again.

Anika couldn't think of a better way of spending the day.

* * * *

Anika noted the sky was turning a luminous blue-black as they got out of bed. They'd missed everything he'd suggested they do and she couldn't have cared less.

There was a knock at the door that Luca answered while she ducked into the bathroom.

A few minutes later, he rapped at the door before sticking his head in. "I have a surprise for you."

He pushed open the door and revealed a stack of boxes. She noted the names on the boxes. He'd had clothes brought up from the boutique to surprise her.

"Luca, you shouldn't have!"

In spite of her words, she crossed the room in a few steps and took them from him, then she headed to the dressing room.

Laughing, he followed. "What do you think?"

"Give me a second." She carefully opened the boxes one by one, starting with the biggest and working her way down. He had thought of everything. The magnificent blue satin gown was as simple as it was gorgeous. The sleeveless bateau-necked dress was form fitting at the top and would graze her hips before flaring in a trailing fishtail hem. That was where the simplicity ended.

A smaller package revealed shoes to match and finally even decadent lingerie to go with the cut of the dress.

Anika's attention fell on the final container. She knew whatever was in the signature De Winter box would set off the outfit with glittering accents. When she opened it, she gasped. The sapphire encrusted necklace was from their latest line, La Mer.

He'd even thought of makeup and everything else she might need.

"Well?" He waited, expectation clear on his face.

Anika couldn't hide her enthusiasm. "It's wonderful! I suppose this is a hint to what we'll be doing tonight?"

His small smile turned into a beaming grin. "It might be. So where do you think we're going?"

She mentally ran through the possibilities. They'd already been to the casino, though there could have been an event going on that they could check out. "I don't know. The opera?"

"Right in one." He winked at her. "Need help getting dressed?"

If he helped her there was little chance of them getting out of the suite at all.

Laughing, she waved him out. "Don't you have primping to do too?"

He smirked. "I don't need to primp." And with that, he disappeared into the bedroom.

Anika eyed the clothes. So thoughtful. And perfect.

If he kept this up, he would ruin her for all the other men on the planet. A nagging little voice at the back of her mind whispered, *Hasn't he already?*

She blanked it out and went back to getting dressed. Anika spent extra time on her hair and makeup so she would do the clothes justice. When she finally finished, she stood and looked at herself in the mirror as she reached behind her neck to fasten the heavy necklace. "Not bad."

"I think you're doing yourself an injustice." Luca swept into the room behind her to do the clasp for her. "You look stunning." He looked at her in the mirror and nodded as if he had reached a conclusion about something.

"What?"

"When I found the dress, it stood out to me only because it matches your eyes."

Could he ever say anything wrong? Heat crept into her cheeks. "I noticed you found a shop that sells De Winter jewelry.

"I could hardly let the original De Winter Ice Princess go out in anything else, could I?"

She ran her fingers over the gorgeous diamonds and sapphires set in waves like the sea the collection was named after, watching as they winked back at her under the light. "It's too much. You do realize I know how much these cost."

"I was counting on it." He handed her the earrings, the bracelet and the ring in turn.

"Showing off?" She put them on and looked at herself in the mirror. She couldn't remember the last time she'd worn so much jewelry.

"Not at all. Only trying to match the worth of the woman wearing them." He came up behind her and nipped her shoulder playfully. "As far as I'm concerned, I haven't come close to matching that yet."

Utterly charmed, she let him take her hand and lead her into the bedroom where he pulled a tuxedo jacket off its hanger and put it on. Luca straightened his tie and held out his arms for her appraisal. "Do I look good enough to escort you to the opera?"

He was so handsome the opera might have to wait.

Luca closed his eyes before opening them again to give her a smoldering look. "Don't look at me like that, *cara*."

She feigned innocence. "Like what?"

"Like you want to devour me," he growled. "It's hard enough motivating myself to leave the suite without you reminding me why we should stay in."

She watched him war with himself a while before she decided she should take the lead. "Come on. It will still be here afterward."

He grumbled something that sounded like grudging assent and let her drag him out through the door.

They climbed into the limo that waited for them at the curb and settled in for the ride. Anika watched Luca from the corner of her eye, wondering what was going through his mind. He stared out of the window for a long while before he turned to return her gaze.

For a second, his eyes were so dark, so pensive, she didn't know what to think. Then he simply slid his hand into hers, interlocking their fingers. That one little gesture was more telling, more intimate, than anything he could say. It was surprising, considering how they'd filled the day. They'd explored every inch of each other and yet the touch of his palm against hers... It filled her with warmth. For the first time, it was more than just sex.

Anika shoved that thought aside in favor of analyzing what was in front of her. Of course, they fit together, her hand was pale compared to his olive complexion but they complemented each other. Hadn't they proven over the past few days that they fit together physically?

She wanted to pull her hands free of his, but the sensation was enough to keep hers interlocked with his.

When Anika looked to Luca, she found his gaze riveted on their linked fingers as well. As if he hadn't been the one to initiate the contact and was surprised to find they were joined.

Luca rubbed his thumb over the back of her hand, slowly, thoughtfully. His attention was drawn back to her face and he narrowed his eyes speculatively. His smile spread gradually over his sensuous mouth. "You know what we could be doing right now?"

The many differently possibilities had crossed her mind, but his imagination was probably much more interesting than what was in her head. "What could we do that we haven't already done today?"

His grin widened at her challenge. Luca kept hold of her hand and leaned in close but made no contact with any other part of her. His breath brushed hot over her cheek when he whispered, "First I would stand you in the middle of the room so I could see all your beautiful body. I would circle you, taking a good look at what's mine." Luca's voice dropped huskily. "And you are *mine*, aren't you Anika?"

Mouth dry, she nodded.

"That's right. Because I was the first one to peel the clothes from you. The first to run his hands, his lips, his tongue over that amazing skin."

Anika's pulse throbbed as she imagined the sensations his touch coaxed from her.

"I would run my thumb over your plump, luscious lips while my other hand would be busy elsewhere. Perhaps in your thick hair. Do you know how wild it makes me to see your hair loose in carefree ebony waves? Or tousled after we've made love for hours?"

She'd had no idea but did her best to get her overstimulated mind to file that fact away to use against him later.

"Maybe my hand will be busy at your breasts, toying with your pretty little nipples. They always seem to be as eager to greet me as I am to feel them against my palm. My lips. And I know by this point, they would be more than ready for my tongue to flick over one before I suck it, drawing that moan from your lips that I love to hear."

She gasped. It was as if he'd actually done as he'd said. Anika could almost feel the heat of his lips on her breasts. But Luca hadn't moved. The liquid pull between her thighs intensified as he kept talking in his gravelly, slightly accented voice.

"Or would my hand be curved around that delicious ass of yours? Do you know how magnificent it is? How distracting? Both hands would be needed there, I think. Cupping, squeezing and feeling those perfect globes."

Anika forgot how to breathe and had to remind her lungs to function as she listened to his hypnotic voice. God, she wanted him. "Luca..."

He ignored her. "By this point you'll be wet for me, yearning for me to touch you where you want me most. But I don't give it to you. I want you to know that no one else can do this to you. That I'm the only one who can work your body like an instrument."

Anika stared at him. He was so close, it would be so easy to lock the doors and get him to show her exactly what he wanted to do with her.

"But I would glide my mouth from your nipple, down over your ribs, your stomach, maybe dip my tongue into your belly button as I make my way to my goal. You will be trembling now. I might be the one kneeling in front of you but I hold all the power. You know where I'm going. Where I'm going to put my mouth. But should I? Or should I draw out your pleasure further? I pause to look up at you. Would you convince me you need my tongue inside you?"

She would tangle her fingers in his hair and drag him to her.

"If I know you as well as I think I do, you would, in no uncertain terms, figure out a way to convince me. Let it never be said that I don't know how to play nice. I would let you direct me. After all, we have the same goal."

Luca shifted, not budging any closer but his mouth brushed her earlobe, sending shockwaves of heat radiating through her.

"I would part your folds and taste you. You have no idea how sweet you are—or how addictive. I could spend the rest of my life with my face buried between your thighs." He grazed her earlobe again. "You taste like ambrosia."

Anika clutched his hand.

"I grip your ass and hold you to me as I lick and taste at my leisure."

She let her eyes drift close as the images and the sensations that accompanied them washed over her.

"Your greedy clit is hard against my tongue, wanting as much attention as I'm willing to give it. But I ignore it for the moment. Instead, I'd part your thighs and plunge my fingers into you. Gently. Teasingly. Finding that spot that makes you writhe against me."

Luca placed his hand on her knee and she jolted as if he had done what he'd said.

"You're so hot and wet. And snug around my fingers. It makes me imagine what it would be like to be deep inside you. Having you tight around me. That makes my cock harden even more. I know I'm on the verge, but I want to hear you sing for me. Just once before I sink into you."

Breathless, Anika trembled from head to toe.

"So I drive my fingers deep and suck your clit into my mouth." He paused and he closed his hand on her knee lowering his head so his mouth was a breath away. "And you come for me."

And she did. Like an overinflated balloon, she burst. Luca closed his mouth over hers to muffle her keening cries. Anika clung to Luca. Fireworks burst in her vision as she felt her panties moistened more and her dress was probably visibly ruined. It took her a little while to come back down to earth but when she did, she stared at him in awe as she caught her breath. His words and voice were all it took for her to see stars.

"Do you want to hear what happens next?" he drawled.

"I'd rather experience it." She regretted leaving the hotel room. They should have just locked themselves in for the duration of the stay and never re-emerged.

He didn't even bother to hide the smug, self-satisfied expression on his face. "See? You should listen to me more often."

If he kept telling her stories like the one he just had, she would be glad to do it. There was no reason why they couldn't continue a relationship by phone... Anika berated herself for what she was thinking.

She had never imagined someone could fill her consciousness so completely. That there would be someone she couldn't keep her hands off or stop thinking about. It was a heady thing — and temporary. Anika kept reminding herself. It was fine for the moment, but once she went back to her life, she would go back to being the Ice Princess again.

Why didn't that thought make her as happy as it used to?

The rest of the limo ride to the opera was short, thankfully. When they pulled up to the curb, Luca removed his hand from her thigh, where it had been steadily climbing, and took hers to help her out.

They streamed into the opera house, which was part of the casino, with countless others. Several voices called out Luca's name. He nodded in greeting, but didn't budge from her side when they beckoned him over. She noticed quite a few of them were women and even caught the glaring eye of a couple of ladies Anika shrugged them off. They could think what they liked about her. It wasn't as if she had to spend any time with any of them. Nor did their opinions matter to her.

Luca led the way up to the box and helped her into her plush seat before taking his own. Several others parted the luxurious curtains covering the door to join them, much to Anika's dismay. It seemed teasing him and testing his vaunted control would have to wait.

They settled in, chatting a little with the two couples who had joined them. Truth be told, Anika had little interest in small talk. She forced herself, however. It would never be said that Anika De Winter was a rude woman. Luca was as charming as ever, easily winning over both couples.

When the lights finally dimmed, they directed their attentions to the stage.

It was a vague surprise when dancers in tutus appeared. Anika had been so distracted that she hadn't even asked what they were going to see. She would have enjoyed an opera, but she loved ballet.

Not long after the overture had echoed away, Luca threaded his fingers with hers, toying with them a moment before his hand comfortably held hers on his rock-hard thigh. His gaze never left the stage, and yet he had found her hand as easily as if it was his own.

Was it so surprising after the past few days?

Anika toed off her shoe, knowing no one would notice under the length of her dress, and slid it up his trouser leg as far as she could go. He tensed, but other than that, she could see no other reaction. Wriggling her toes against his hair roughened calf, she could barely make out his jaw clenching in the near darkness.

He retaliated by inching her hand up his thigh to meet his growing erection then stroking it with the back of her hand.

Muscles tight, Anika refused to look away from the stage, afraid she would draw attention to what he was doing. The feel of him, hot and hard, through the fabric of his trousers made her shiver with delight and anticipation.

"Are you cold, *cara*?" he asked mildly. As if he didn't know what had caused her reaction. Luca took off his jacket and covered her shoulders with it, much to the delight of the other women in the box. He tugged her closer, securing an arm around her waist.

It wasn't until the others returned their gazes to the stage that it dawned on Anika the ulterior motive of him giving her his coat—it hid is hand. The one he currently slid up her side to cup her breast. He molded her gently, squeezing and weighing. He lightly pinched her pebbled nipple through the fabric before grazing it with the nail of his thumb. The sensation rocketed straight to her core. Anika fought to keep still, to stop the moan that built in her throat from escaping and scandalizing everyone around them.

Returning her hand to his groin, she found him at full mast, straining against the zipper of his fly. Anika so wanted to give into the urge to unzip and reach inside, but she knew the rasp of the zipper would be heard. It was bad enough that they could be caught any second behaving like a couple of hormone-crazed idiots.

It didn't stop her from curling her hand around him and stroking him firmly. She heard him exhale, felt his hand grip her breast tightly for an instant. Anika continued. She traced the veins along his length to the broad head, circling it lightly before gliding back down. She delighted in the shivers her light strokes elicited from him. She grew bolder, closing a hand around him and pumping his cock firmly.

He gripped her hand to stop her. Luca leaned over and muttered, "I should have bought you a short strapless dress. At least then I could touch you." His thumb traced her aching nipple. "Or better yet, we should have stayed in the suite."

Hindsight, they said, was twenty-twenty.

Stuck in their seats for the duration, Anika did everything she could not to make a noise while he teased and fondled her. She, in return, did her best to make him relent. Her opponent, it seemed, was just as stubborn as she was.

By the time the performance ended, Anika was practically a puddle in her seat, trembling and breathless. Luca didn't move but bid goodbye to the others as they vacated the box. Anika only turned to smile and wave as they left.

The moment the door clicked closed, Luca reacted.

Quick as lightning, he dragged her from the seat and pressed her into the curtains obscuring the door. Tangling his hands in her hair, Luca plundered her mouth with his.

He lifted his head, drawing a ragged breath. "You know how hard it was to sit through that with your hot hand wrapped my around my cock?" he growled.

Luca wrenched her skirt, hiking it up around her waist. He gripped her thigh with one hand and freed himself with the other. With a yank, he tore lace and silk aside to thrust into her as he bit her shoulder.

Anika clawed his shoulders, trying to pull him closer as he pounded into her. She was slick and more than ready for him, but the stretch of his invasion hitched the breath in her lungs. The friction of skin on skin was exquisite in counterpart with the slide of the silk against her. She could smell her own arousal mingled with the mouthwatering scent of him. He leaned back so she could see his thick cock, glistening with her juices plunging in and out of her. Luca watched them for a moment before his gaze met hers. As far as sex went, it was animalistic. Hard and fast and breathless. Complete and utter madness. And incredibly satisfying. Having Luca wild and uninhibited was better than she could imagine.

He thrust into her, taking everything she gave and demanding more. Growling into the crook of her neck, biting and sucking, he plunged deep, keeping his grip tight on her hips. It took him mere minutes to bring her to the fastest and most knee-buckling orgasm to date. Muffling her cries with his hand, Luca kept up the pace and followed with a low groan seconds later, leaving them satiated and trembling as they clung to each other.

Still deep inside Anika, feeling the aftershocks rack her slender frame, Luca fought to catch his breath. That had been crazy. Had he been thinking with anything other than his cock, he wouldn't have pounced on her like some horny beast. She deserved better than half-dressed rutting in a public place — but it had been damn good.

It wasn't until he pulled out that the euphoria gave way to self-recrimination. He fought back a groan at the exquisite sensation of her tender skin caressing his cock.

Condom!

He must have been out of his mind to forget the condom.

Sex in public and without protection. He cursed himself for being so careless.

Voices headed down the corridor toward them and from the panic on her face, Anika heard them too.

They quickly righted their clothes and after a moment to breathe, exited the box. Luca berated himself the entire trek through the building. Inhaling the fresh air helped him clear his head a little.

"Luca? Are you okay?" Anika looked paler than usual. Her expression was dazed and yet, at the same time, pinched.

"Not really." He took her hand and turned her to face him. "I apologize. My behavior…"

She squeezed his hand. "It wasn't like I tried to stop you."

She was so sweet. Something in his chest clutched as he dove ahead.

"Anika…are you on birth control?" Luca couldn't believe he was having this conversation. The strange part was the longer he thought about it, the less the possibility worried him. A baby with Anika… He gritted his teeth. He couldn't force something like that on her. It was something they should discuss before…before he was an idiot and forgot the condom. "I'm so sorry. I've never lost control like that before."

Her eyes widened when comprehension dawned. He could almost see her mind furiously working. "No. Until I met you, I didn't exactly have the need. We should be fine, though. I hope. If all the things I've read in women's magazine are right, that is. I can't get pregnant…oh God…I don't know what part of my cycle I'm in…"

It was the first time he'd seen her truly nervous. And babbling. He pulled her in to hold her close. "We'll figure it out—together."

It was the way she looked at him—the complete trust that emerged from behind the panic and fear—that something inside fell into place.

Anika De Winter was *the* one.

And the fact scared the hell out of him.

Chapter Nine

The following morning, Luca got out of bed before she woke, left her a brief note and went for a run. The first time he'd done that in months, maybe even a year.

The punishing run was just what he needed to clear his head, and by the time he'd rounded the corner back to the hotel, he'd reached several conclusions.

One, he was never going to run again. Two, he would feel out Anika and find out if she felt the same about him before revealing his true feelings for her. Three, if she didn't reciprocate his feelings, he would find a way to convince Anika he was *the* one for her.

There was no point in revealing his hand without knowing what she had in hers. Luca knew she felt something for him. No one could give themselves as completely as she did if she didn't feel it too.

But he had to be sure.

He was careful in all areas of his life—until Anika showed up—and it had helped him become the success he was now.

It would help him in this case as well.

And if there was a baby... There was no way he was going to let her walk away with his child. The thought made his chest hurt. He couldn't let his child grow up without his or her father.

He stopped by the restaurant on his way and picked up some croissants and coffee.

Luca hated the uncertainty, not knowing how she felt, or the possible repercussions of their interlude at the opera. He wasn't even sure how Anika would be when he got back to the suite.

The night before, they'd returned, had fallen asleep in each other's arms and he'd felt whole. For the first time in his life, he didn't feel as though there was a gaping hole in his chest. The missing part of him he'd been trying to replace for years with money, women and fast cars was now filled to overflowing with Anika.

It was no wonder nothing was ever enough. Anika was more than he could ever hope for or had expected to come into his life.

And he had blackmailed her into spending time with him. Though it had worked out, he wanted to start anew.

He smiled when he realized he'd been calling her pet names in Italian for a couple of days at least. Apparently, his heart worked faster than his head.

Chuckling, he tiptoed up the stairs. Not knowing if she was awake yet, he crept into the bedroom to find her still sound asleep.

Curled on her side, she looked angelic with her hair spread over the pillow, her face relaxed, unmarred by any worry. She said he seemed happier lately. He could say the same about her. When he first laid eyes on her, Anika looked as though she carried the weight of the world on her slender shoulders. Perhaps she did. He'd done a little digging into her family and knew of the financial troubles they'd had. He also knew that she had been the one to turn things around for them. It had been slow, but the results were now becoming noticeable.

Anika's influence on the PR of the De Winter Group was masterful. It impressed him.

He had investigated a bit on the ex-fiancé as well. As far as he was concerned, Joshua Rhys-Jones wasn't worthy of her — would never be. He never believed he could be thankful at another's misfortune, especially Anika's, but he was glad that the pathetic excuse of a man had run out on his own wedding.

He stroked his finger down her smooth cheek, marveling at the creamy texture of her skin.

Her thick lashes fluttered as they opened to reveal her incredible eyes. Bleary as they were, they focused on him immediately and a smile turned her lips. "What time is it?"

He held up the tray and lifted the lid so she could see what he'd brought. "Time for breakfast."

When she stretched, the sheet slipped dangerously low almost driving all thoughts of food from his mind.

Smiling, she hitched the sheet around her breasts and pushed herself up to sit against her pillow. "You know if you keep feeding me this way, I'll expect it all the time."

If it would make her happy, he'd do it gladly. He winked and offered her the tray to let her have her pick of the croissants.

She took one, eyeing him as she did so. "So you run, huh?"

He nodded at the paper on his pillow. "I left you a note but I obviously made it back before you woke."

"Thanks." She took a bite of her pastry and sighed. "These are so buttery."

Luca took a bite to see for himself and agreed. "Yes and yes. Though I haven't run in a while and I probably won't again for a long time."

She laughed. "So what brought on the self-abuse?"

"I needed to do some thinking. Rather than wake you, I thought I would run. It was something I've enjoyed in the past and haven't done in far too long."

Her smile faded. "Thinking about what happened last night?"

He took her hand but it lay limp in his. "Among other things."

"Look, I know it was stupid. That we just got caught up in the moment. But I don't regret it." She dropped her gaze from his. "If anything should…happen…there are options…"

Luca's vision blurred for an instant before it was veiled with red. "And you've considered all the options?"

His grip tightened on her hand, until Anika had to tug it from his grasp. "Haven't you?"

Luca grabbed her by the shoulders. "Not the option of getting rid of my child, I haven't!"

Anika stared at him. "I never said I would."

Did he have any clue just how freaked out she was? How a baby would change everything? And yet that option had been imagined and summarily discounted. She could never bring herself to do it, no matter how drastically a child would change her life. How he or she would tie her to Luca forever.

After he said he would stand by her no matter what the outcome, she had relaxed a little, telling herself that as long as he was with her, she could get through anything. But now?

She shoved him back, got out of the bed and picked up what clothes she could find and threw them on. It didn't matter whose.

"Anika..."

"Back off, Luca." She trembled from head to toe and had put on his shirt from the night before. And she didn't care. She grabbed her shoes, but when she couldn't find the other one, she fought the urge to throw the one she held at his head. "I need time to think too."

He held his hands up. "Anika, I'm sorry. I'm just stressed. I don't know how to handle this—us." He turned his dark brown eyes to her. "I'm never been in...this deep with anyone before."

In as deep? Of course, he'd been so careful with his past lovers he'd never had to deal with this sort of situation before. Why had she let him in? She had seen all the signs. He'd played her and she had let him walk all over her.

"You don't think I'm stressed?" She dropped the shoe. "You have no idea what I'm going through." Anika strode for the door when what she wanted to do was run for it. She needed to get out before she started crying and she refused to do it in front of him.

Luca got in the way, of course. He held out his trousers and her shoes. "Anika."

"Don't touch me." She ignored the clothes and stepped just out of reach when he tried to put his hands on her shoulders. The tears threatened to well, but she ruthlessly fought them back. It hurt so much to fight him. To war with herself. All she wanted to do was fall into his arms and let him make the world right again. But she knew that only happened in fairy tales. Anika had gotten herself into the situation and she would deal with it. Like everything else in her life. She would do it on her own.

He held up his hands and let her pass. "All I ask is that we talk once you've calmed down."

At the moment, she wasn't sure she would never relax again. "I've got to go."

Luca reluctantly stepped aside. "Of course. Don't forget me, *cara*."

The elevator doors closed.

Anika willed the elevator to descend faster. When the doors parted, she ran to her suite not caring who saw her. Thankfully, there weren't many people around to notice a crying mess dashing through the halls.

She locked herself in the suite for the rest of the day so she could think, panic and think a little more. Periodically, there would be a knock at the door and on the other side would be a porter with something from Luca. First came her partially eaten breakfast. Her appetite had abandoned her, so it stayed that way. While she stood on the verandah staring out at the ocean, there was another delivery—the clothing and jewels from the night before. The final knock brought a note, handwritten in clean economic script that could only be Luca's, asking to meet for dinner in the restaurant.

What could it hurt? She was drained, but calm. They needed to talk. She had been overly emotional, then again, how could she not be? As long as he didn't push her she would more than likely remain that way.

Anika prepared for the meal as she would any business meeting. She dressed in white blouse and black suit. She wore a touch of makeup on her lips and cheeks. Just to give herself some color. She wound her hair into a bun low on the back of her head, to keep it out of her way. She deliberately chose sky high heels to boost her confidence. She mentally prepared arguments for all the scenarios she could imagine.

But as she stared at her pale face and pink, still-swollen eyes, she knew she wouldn't fool anyone—especially not Luca.

Giving up, she grabbed her purse, and fought to make sure she looked calm, although inside she couldn't be more tumultuous.

Anika almost talked herself out of meeting with him twice before she got to the restaurant. She knew she was being ridiculous. What's the worst that could happen?

Taking a deep fortifying breath, she walked into the bustling restaurant.

Luca was at a corner table, watching the door with an uncharacteristic look of uncertainty on his face. He stood the moment he caught sight of her, a tremulous smile slanting his mouth.

"I was afraid you wouldn't come." His gaze raked over her taking in her attire. "Dressed for battle I see."

"Not at all." She took the seat he pulled out for her.

"You look wonderful, just the same." Luca slipped into the seat across from her, his expression somewhat hopeful. "Would you like anything to drink?"

"Ice water will be fine."

He nodded and waved the waiter over, ordered Anika's water and asked for one of his own then sent the slightly perplexed man away.

Luca reached his hands across the table, palms up, and waited for her to react however she chose. She placed her hands in his. He closed his around hers with a small smile. "I'm sorry about earlier. I shouldn't have raised my voice. I shouldn't have—"

"Luca Rossi!"

The feminine squeal came from the entrance and drew curious glances from around the room.

Luca looked at a loss, but his confusion quickly turned into chagrin when a beautiful blonde bounced toward the table chased by the harassed-looking maître d'.

"I haven't seen you in ages!"

"Chantelle... How nice to see you."

From his choked expression, Anika figured he was anything but.

She grabbed a chair from the nearest table.

The poor man trying to keep order in his restaurant protested, "Mademoiselle, please. I can arrange —"

"Nonsense. I can just squeeze in here." Waving him away, she shoved the chair in next to Luca's and crammed herself into it. The maître d' only relented when Luca nodded to him. He scurried away, his face red as though he was about to burst.

It was only once she was seated that she seemed to notice Anika. Instead of introducing herself, she turned to bewildered man at the opposite end of the table. "Luca, don't tell me you're in Monaco for business. Don't you ever have fun?"

Anika turned to Luca, waiting for his answer, or for him to say anything, really.

"Chantelle, this is Anika —"

"Oh, my goodness!" she exclaimed. Fanning the air around her face, she bounced in her seat. "You're the De Winter Ice Princess!"

At least their PR was working. "I am." She gave her the best smile she could muster, but the oblivious woman's enthusiasm wasn't to be contained and it irked the hell out of Anika.

"Your ads are amazing! And so is the jewelry! I would die if someone bought me anything from your store."

"Maybe one day," Anika said mildly.

Chantelle smiled coquettishly at Luca and ran her finger down his arm. "Hopefully one day soon." Her gaze ping-ponged between them. "I did interrupt your meeting, didn't I? Luca are you getting into business with the De Winters? If you do, does that mean you get a discount?" She batted her lashes at him with wide-eyed hopefulness.

Anika rubbed her temple, watching as Luca tried to extricate himself from the grasp of the woman next to him.

"Chantelle, we're in the middle of something."

She pouted. "But I haven't seen you in such a long time—"

"Why don't I leave you two to catch up?" Anika stood and picked up her purse. "I'll be back in a minute." She didn't know why she added that bit when she wasn't sure if she was coming back or not.

"Anika." Luca looked at her imploringly, but whether it was an entreaty to stay or to help him get rid of their unwanted tablemate, she wasn't sure.

Either way, she wasn't interested. "I'll be right back."

She wove her way through to the powder room. Dropping her purse on the plush chair just inside, Anika glared at herself in the mirror. If she stayed with Luca, how often would something like this happen? She should just walk out and get on with her life. Forget that any of this came to pass.

Anika paced the length of the room. He had seemed so happy to see her and earnest about making things right between them. Though he had barely managed to say anything before the deranged Barbie doll ambushed them.

She had to give him a chance at least. He had been less than happy to see the woman. It was no wonder why, Chantelle was like a hyperactive Chihuahua. If that was the type of woman he was into, they had nothing left to say. Anika couldn't—wouldn't—become like that for anyone.

Sighing, she stared back at the woman in the mirror. The one who reflected was her but at the same time not. Familiar but different in so many ways.

What would she look like after she returned to her life?

Anika wasn't sure she wanted to imagine that quite yet. She would give him a chance. Luca deserved that much.

She tidied her makeup and walked back into the restaurant.

* * * *

Well, that could have gone better.

Chantelle couldn't have had worse timing. Or have been more irritating. How had he ever found her attractive? And the look on Anika's face... If getting her to listen to him was going to be a battle before, it was probably near insurmountable now.

That was if she even came back. Luca wanted to believe she was made of tougher stuff than that, but after seeing her, he knew she'd been thinking long and hard about their relationship and her conclusion, if her eyes were anything to go by, wasn't going to please him. Still, she had shown up and given him that chance.

Only for it to be demolished by a woman he barely remembered.

A woman who was practically trying to climb in his lap in the middle of the restaurant. He pushed her gently, but firmly, back. "It was great seeing you again,

Chantelle, but as you can see, I'm in the middle of something important."

Her eyes grew big and glassy. "More important than me?"

Infinitely more so. Though he could hardly say that to her face and not expect her to make more of a spectacle of herself. "Aren't you here with anyone? Perhaps you should find them before they think you've abandoned them?"

"They can wait. Speaking of being abandoned." She looked around in an exaggerated display. "I don't see the Ice Princess anywhere. Maybe you're the one who has been abandoned."

That's what he was afraid of. "Maybe I should go check on her." As Luca stood, he scanned the room, searching for any sign of Anika.

"She'll be back soon enough, I'm sure." She reached out to him, trying to get him to sit again.

Luca pushed aside her grasping hands. Then he saw a familiar figure. She tried to hide the pink hair under a hat but it was unmistakable. The woman behind the blog that had been plaguing him for years. After seeing all the horrible things she'd written about Anika, he knew she had pursued her as well. The woman was a leech. How had she known to follow them here?

She crept in and took a seat by the balcony doors on the other side of the room. She wouldn't have seen Anika leaving but if she came back… He couldn't let her write another trashy piece about Anika.

Luca made a decision. Putting on his most charming smile, he sat and took Chantelle's hand.

He just hoped Anika would forgive him someday.

Anika froze in the doorway when she saw Luca wrap his arm around the blonde and practically drag her into his lap. It took her far too long to process what she saw and force her body to move.

Stumbling back, she strode away as quickly as she could on legs that were weighed down by lead. On autopilot, she walked back up to her suite and gathered her things, leaving behind everything he'd given her and even the things she'd worn while with him.

She carefully piled them in two different stacks and left notes with instructions to return the jewelry to the shop and make sure the clothes went to charity.

Anika grabbed her now near-empty suitcase and dragged it haphazardly behind her as she blindly made her way to reception. She arranged for her instructions to be carried out, for a seat on the next flight back to London and a limo to take her to the airport.

* * * *

A mere three hours later, she stared down at Heathrow below the circling plane. The flight had given her time to reflect, to plan. She should have confronted him. But then what good would that have done? She would have caused a scene — and for what? The end would have been the same. She would still be back in England, and he would be doing whatever it was with whomever he wanted.

Because he didn't want her. And if he didn't, who would? For the first time, she'd let her guard down. Let Luca in to see the real Anika and was found wanting.

The ache in her chest didn't get any better no matter how she spun it. And that was why she didn't do relationships. They were emotional time bombs that only ended in hurt and wasted time.

The trip through the airport and the ride back to her apartment were a blur. London was even grayer than she'd thought possible. The dark clouds that loomed forebodingly over the city seemed to gather over Knightsbridge and, more specifically, her building. Or perhaps they were just following her, drawn by her mood. She shrugged off the fanciful thought. It was time to get back to real life.

Thankfully, the vultures that had been hovering around her before she'd left weren't around. The last thing she needed was to wade through the sea of prying questions and cameras shoved in her face. The paparazzi probably realized she wasn't there and left. At least that was the hope. She more than likely had a day or two tops before they found out she was back. She waved hello to the woman at the desk, picked up her mail and walked into the elevator.

Anika kicked off her shoes the moment she walked through her door, dropping her purse and suitcase down next to them, and sighed with relief. She had bought the apartment just over a year before. Once their company started turning a profit again and she felt they were stable, she jumped at the chance of having her own place. The new development in Knightsbridge seemed right up her alley. It might not have been as prestigious as others nearby but it suited her needs. With one bedroom, an office space, a gorgeous view of the city and situated a few minutes from everything she needed, it was ideal. That, and she didn't have to open the door to anyone she didn't want to.

Her family's home had more of an open-door policy when it came to guests, and growing up, she didn't know what or whom she would run into when she went downstairs. In the apartment, she was guaranteed peace and the space she required.

Putting her mobile phone on speaker, she listened to her messages as she opened the fridge to investigate it. Not that she expected to find much. She pulled out a bottle of water and shut the door again. A grocery trip would have to wait. If she got hungry enough, she would just call for takeout. *No more handsome billionaires waiting ready with food.* The thought triggered a pang of regret.

Her phone rang, but she couldn't be bothered to answer, preferring to stay where she was, brooding and miserable.

"Anika! Answer! I know you're screening!" Petra's voice shouted through the phone.

What impeccable timing. Anika picked it up and swiped the screen. "Hi."

"Hi?" Her friend's voice rose an octave. "That's all you have to say to me?"

Anika jerked the phone away from her ear and kept it at a safe distance. "I just got in. What do you expect me to say to you?"

"How about a thank you for a wonderful vacation?"

"Right. Thanks." She couldn't keep the sarcasm from her voice.

"I called to check up on you and was told you'd left." The laughter in her friend's voice died immediately. "What happened? Was the staff rude? Did they say something about how you got the room?"

Anika ran a hand over her face. "No, nothing like that. I don't really want to get into it right now. I want to have a bath, maybe have something to eat and get in bed."

"Nothing happened. Right."

Petra was like a pit bull when she wanted to get to the heart of something. Anika searched her mind for an excuse to get off the line before she spilled everything and had to listen to her friend try to make sense of it when she could barely understand what she'd gotten herself into. "I had a long day all right? The flight took it out of me."

"It's barely a flight from Nice to London, so that's a load of bull. So what really happened?"

Rolling her eyes, Anika sighed. "I met a gorgeous billionaire who blackmailed me into spending time with him. Only the more time we spent together, the more I liked him. We had a passionate few days spent mostly naked, but he turned out to be a womanizing jerk, so I left." She sighed before adding, "Oh yeah, and I might be pregnant as a result."

There was a moment of silence then a huff. "You don't have to be a cow about it. If you don't want to tell me then don't. If you don't want to talk then will you at least listen to what I've been up to?"

Anika had half expected her friend not to believe the story. It was so out of character for her, she knew it sounded like a complete fabrication. Only it *had* happened, as much as she wished it hadn't. It would have been nice to have someone to talk to about it.

She listened to Petra prattle on about what had been going on in her life. Only half of it made it through the haze that clouded Anika's mind, however. Most of her thoughts dwelled on the last image she had of Luca and the blonde. Why had he invited her to dinner if that was how he was going to act? Was it a ploy to get her to walk out him? What was the point? Trying to make sense of the thoughts careening through her head made her want to scream and cry and hurtle things at the wall. Nothing made sense.

"Are you listening to me?"

Anika sniffed, aware she was mere seconds away from turning into a blubbering mess "Yeah, of course."

"What was I saying, then?"

What had she been talking about? Anika didn't have a clue. "To be honest, I don't know. I wasn't kidding when I said I wasn't feeling great, Petra. I think I'm coming down with something."

"Well, why didn't you say so? Get a cuppa down you and call me tomorrow. If I don't hear from you, I'm calling the militia."

That made her smile a little. "I don't think they make house calls."

"They will if I make the call." Her voice softened. "Feel better, okay?"

"I'll try."

They said their goodbyes and Anika hung up. If she'd known that was all she had to say she would have said it sooner. It had been nice to hear from her friend, though.

Forgoing the food, she walked into her bathroom and started a bath only to hear her phone ringing in the other room. It was probably Petra again, so Anika dashed back out to reassure her she would be fine. The last thing she needed was a surprise visit from her old friend and getting involved in yet another of her schemes.

"I'll be fine, Petra. I just need some rest."

"That's wonderful to hear that you're fine, dear. Even though I had to find out that you were back in the country via a gossip blog," sniped a familiar voice.

"Hello, Mother." Anika sagged into the nearest chair and dropped her head into her hand. "That was quick. They must be getting better at tracking me."

"Or you're slipping. You looked awful by the way. Would it be too much to ask to run a brush through your hair before you traipse through an airport?"

So that's how they saw her. The airport. Looked like her solitude was going to disappear a lot quicker than she'd expected.

"Did you at least have a good time after abandoning us to clear up after your mess?"

Trust her mother to make it sound as if she cared and didn't in the same breath.

"It was fine. And it's not *my* mess to clean up. You, Dad and the Rhys-Joneses pushed for the wedding. Joshua just had the sense to run." Anika winced, knowing she was going to get a lecture about duty and just how much they relied on the wedding to turn things around for the family.

"That's a fine thing to say to your mother."

"Tell me it isn't true."

"That's neither here nor there. We need you to make an appearance at a meeting in a few days' time. Can you make it? Or will you be hiding from the paparazzi in Cairo or something next time something upsets you?"

Anika rubbed the space between her brows. "Why do I have to be there?"

"We have a new investor on the line. We thought it would be best for him to meet everyone. You know, show a united front. I can count on you to be there for the family, right?"

"Yes. Whatever. Text me the time and place." Anything to get her off the phone.

"Good. And I expect you'll be a great deal more enthusiastic when we meet. This is important."

As was everything that involved the De Winter name. Anika hung up. Her phone trilled a moment later, probably with the details of the meeting. She'd look at it later.

She returned to the bathroom just in time to save the room from a minor flooding. Sopping up the excess water with a heap of towels, she emptied it a little and got in the tub, ignoring the fact that when she did, more water sloshed over the sides.

Closing her eyes, Anika willed herself to forget.

As if she could wipe Luca Rossi from her mind that easily.

* * * *

Far too early the next morning, Anika got up to spend most of her time reorganizing her closet, figuring out what needed to be replaced. She called her assistant with a list of groceries since she really wasn't up to doing the run herself. It was something she hated to do, but she didn't trust the delivery people not to gossip about her purchases. Not that she ever made salacious buys, Anika just didn't want to have another thing to worry about.

She then did the rounds on her laptop to the websites of her favorite boutiques to replenish her clothing. She even tried a bit of yoga to relax, but she just didn't seem able to shake the fatigue or tension no matter how hard she tried to snap out of it. Not all that surprising considering she barely managed to get any sleep.

She arrived at the building ready to get back to business. At least that's what she kept telling herself. The sooner she got her head back in the game, the better. Doing her best to appear as if she had everything in control, Anika caught the pitying glances of some as she made her way through. It took her far too long to connect them not to Luca, but to Joshua.

They pitied her because her fiancé had walked out on her, not because of the devastating man who had broken her heart after just a few days of bliss.

Was it wrong that she felt the loss of a man she barely knew more keenly than the abandonment of a man at the altar? If anyone found out, it was sure to make her look even more heartless than her reputation already made her out to be.

With her back ramrod straight the entire day, Anika went about her business as if she'd never been gone. By the time she got into the elevator, she had everything sorted exactly as it needed to be, though it took her nearly to nine p.m. to get it done right.

On her way to the elevator, she ran into her father, which was not all surprising since he often stayed late as well.

"Anika." He pecked her on the cheek as the doors closed them inside the box.

"Hi, Dad."

"How was your trip?"

She shrugged "It was fine. I wish I'd had longer."

"Don't we all?" He studied her a moment and obviously ascribed her appearance to the same thing everyone else had—her failed nuptials. "I'm sorry about Joshua."

Anika wasn't but she was hardly in the mood to get into that conversation. "Thanks."

"I mean about all of it. We never should have asked you to go through with it." He took her hand. "We'll find another way."

It was the first time he'd ever admitted he was wrong about anything, and Anika was touched he'd apologized. She kissed him on the cheek. "I'm actually glad Joshua ran."

"As am I. The boy is weak. To tell the truth, I didn't think I could handle staring at that face over the table at holidays."

Anika laughed, her heart a little lighter. "Mum called yesterday. She said there's a meeting with an investor in a few days." She was positive the new deal in the making was why her father was in such a forgiving mood.

He nodded. "I'm sure she's told you that we'd like you to be there."

"She was a bit more direct. My presence is required, apparently."

The doors parted. "It would be wonderful if you could make it. It's a bit touch and go. We could use you to sweet talk him," he said laughingly.

Sweet talk. Right. She would be there with her signature statistics and charts. "I'll be there."

Her father smiled. "Great. Need a ride?"

Shaking her head, she smiled. "I'll see you soon."

He pressed his lips to the top of her head and waved goodbye as he strode to the waiting car.

Was her father getting soft in his old age? She laughed at the thought. Not likely. She wandered through the lobby, keeping an eye out for paparazzi outside. Thankfully, there were none. At least none she could see.

There was one thing she'd wanted to do all day but hadn't had the chance, and it wasn't something she was going to send her assistant out to do. Now seemed as good of a time as any since there were no prying eyes around.

Her Ferrari sat in its bay waiting for her, but taking such an extravagant car out would draw unwanted attention. Besides, she wasn't going far.

A brisk walk up the street took her to a corner shop and an even quicker scavenge around the shop led to her goal. She quickly snatched it up, paid and dashed back out again. Straight to her car and back to her apartment, her mind reeling the entire way.

She dropped everything but the little bag at the door. And for a long moment, she simply stood weighing the odds, trying to figure out if she should wait. In the end, she pulled out the box that held the three pregnancy tests.

It had to be too soon to tell. But with each second that ticked by, the possibility seemed to scream louder and louder, becoming more concrete in her mind.

Anika just needed some reassurance. Only she had no idea what result would actually make her feel better.

She read the literature that came in the box twice to make sure she understood correctly. It recommended waiting six to twelve days after her period was due. She tried to do the math but with everything whirling around in her head, she could only conclude that her period was expected in the coming week. Insanity would have claimed her by then, surely.

Putting the tests in the medicine cabinet in her bathroom, Anika took a deep breath and set her phone to alert her when the six days was up.

Like she would need reminding.

She flopped onto the couch and grabbed the remote. Maybe there would be something on to distract her for a while.

Chapter Ten

The next morning she woke with a crick in her neck from her awkward position on the sofa and crankier than usual as a result. She'd never been a morning person, but the cheerful glare of the sun in her eyes was even more annoying than she'd ever remembered it. Anika scowled, checked her phone and groaned.

Not enough time for breakfast, she dashed for the shower. The last thing she needed was to be late on her second day back from what should have been her honeymoon. Anika would grab a coffee at the office and call for breakfast if time allowed. Maybe brunch.

She checked in with her assistant on the way to the office and made sure she was mentally ready for the various meetings, calls and whatever else required her attention. People could gossip all they wanted about her personal life, but on the business side of things, she wasn't giving them any fodder.

The De Winters Group was doing better than they had in the past few years, but they were a long way from being as illustrious as they once had been. With the PR reins in her hands, public relations would not be the weak chain in the link.

It was nonstop from the moment she walked into the building, and her assistant handed her coffee. Between her checking in and actually arriving—apparently there had been a few changes to her schedule, but nothing she couldn't handle. Mail had been sorted and Anika was given the most pressing before she stepped into the elevator. By the time she arrived at her office, she had finished the coffee and was ready to face the day head on.

She cleared her desk of all the work that didn't require consultations or calls before midday. Her lunch meeting was moved to the next day, so she made calls during that time. All that was left was the conference that would end the day. She stared at the schedule on the screen and sighed. The appointment with the investor had been moved ahead, and instead of giving her the evening to prepare, she only had a few hours.

Anika called her assistant and cancelled her meal order. It would take all her concentration to create a presentation that would have their visitors throwing money at the DWG for the foreseeable future.

By the time the meeting came around, Anika was sure she had made a presentation worth being proud of. She had her facts straight, sorted and organized. Everything was clear, precise and very attractive for a prospective investor. All she needed to do was make sure she was on her game. After a quick stop in her private bathroom to retouch her hair and makeup, before she headed to the boardroom, she would be ready.

Much easier said than done. She looked worn. Her skin was so pale makeup would do nothing to hide the dark circles under her eyes. She did her best, however, using every skill she'd ever learned to make herself look somewhat less like a zombie. Her hair lay limp so she pulled it back into a no nonsense bun. It was her usual style when it came to work functions, anyway.

She forced a smile on her face and rolled her eyes. She was trying too hard. Nothing would send investors running faster than someone who reeked of desperation. The cool confidence of the Ice Princess would do the trick. Besides, it had always worked for her before, why change a good thing?

Because she wanted to be the happy, smiling Anika she had been when she was in Monaco. Only the woman reflected back at her looked sad and only reminded her of what she walked away from.

A liar. A cheat. Luca Rossi was a lying cheat.

Anika chanted it to herself like a mantra as she grabbed her laptop, tablet and phone and headed toward the elevators.

She fought back a sigh when she ran into her mother at the end of the corridor. She'd clearly been heading for her office and stopped with a critical glance at her clothing.

"Anika, dear." Isabella De Winter smiled at her daughter, linking her arm through Anika's free one, making sure she had nowhere to run. "Glad you decided to join us."

Anika fought not to roll her eyes. "You asked so nicely for me to be there, how could I say no?"

"You could have at least tried to make an effort. I know you're a little down after the whole wedding fiasco, but you shouldn't let the whole world know."

Anika was too tired to argue. All she wanted to do was get through the next couple hours and maybe convince whoever they were about to see to invest as much as she could coax out of them into their company.

"Who are we seeing? You never did tell me."

He mother rolled eyes that matched hers. "If you would talk to me for more than a minute at a time, I might have been able to brief you."

"I need to be briefed? You said you wanted help convincing an investor." She held up her pile of devices. "I've got everything right here" — she tapped her temple — "and here."

She smoothed her daughter's hair. "I have no doubt, but it never hurts to have a beautiful woman to deliver the information."

Anika's head was throbbing in earnest now. "So who is it you're trying to sell me off to now?"

"That's a repugnant thing to say." Isabella scowled at her. "We're meeting with ALR Venture Capital. I admit I don't know much about them besides their CEO has more money than he knows what to do with, but he is incredibly picky about where they invest their funds."

"Sounds like a smart man." Anika bit the inside of her cheek. A smart man with more money than he knew what to do with? It sounded like a certain handsome Italian.

Anika bit her tongue when she wanted to ask more about the CEO. She let her mother drag her to the boardroom door, unsure if she was eager or dreading what she would find on the other side.

Her breath stuck in her throat when the doors were pushed open. The small team of men and women on the other side stood when they walked in. None was even close to the man who left a hole in her heart.

She took the pang in her gut as relief, because what else could it be?

Anika sucked in a deep breath, gathered herself and dove in.

* * * *

It went well. She knew she had the woman and one of the men by the end of it. The other wasn't a soft touch, but Anika got the feeling that he was waiting for something. For what, she had no clue. A song and a dance? Anika had presented everything in enough detail to catch the eye of anyone with an interest in working with them. If he were waiting for a more…personal enticement, he would just have to keep waiting.

Roland De Winter stood. "Thank you, Anika." He looked around the table. Anika's father was very good at reading expressions. Just like she could see on his face he wasn't completely happy with the result, either. "Well, I think we've talked business long enough. Why don't we take a break? How does dinner sound?"

Anika checked her phone. It was well after seven and she was feeling the effects of skipping every meal. Subsisting on coffee wasn't exactly a good idea — especially considering the circumstances.

She fought her hand away from her abdomen. Just the thought of possibly being pregnant made her head reel more. Who would the baby look like? Wrestling her imagination away from visions of a chubby baby boy who looked like Luca proved to be a bit harder to do.

"Anika?"

Her mother's voice helped bring her back to reality. "Sorry?"

"Are you going to join us?"

"Yes. I'll meet you. Where are you planning on going?"

Her mother gave her the time and place, and Anika nodded. "Right. I'll take my car. See you soon."

Anika waved goodbye to the others. Not much more was needed since they were going to sit down to a meal soon. She headed back to her office and gathered her things. At least a dinner out with her parents would take the monotony out of her night. Though, she had the feeling that later she would be wishing she hadn't gone.

She had some time to kill, so Anika went home to change into something a little less business like in an attempt to feel like the woman she had been just days before.

Nothing too extravagant, of course, just a simple little black dress since she didn't feel the need for color. Black heels. Her hair was brushed, quickly wrapped around a curling iron to combat the limpness and left in loose waves around her shoulders. She allowed some color in her makeup on her lips and cheeks.

She gave her reflection a critical onceover. The woman in the mirror looked better, but still a far cry from the vibrant woman she wanted to be.

One step at a time.

She grabbed a handful of grapes on her way out of the door for a little energy. She would get over him.

Even if she had to keep walking the rest of her life.

* * * *

The restaurant was gorgeous, stuffed to the gills with elegant-looking people and even better-looking food. As she was led to meet the rest of her party, Anika caught a glance at the nearly packed table. She hadn't taken that long, had she? But as it was, there was still one seat after hers that left vacant. A quick tally of the others let her know it was the woman who was missing. What was her name again?

It should have been easy to remember names. She never forgot a name or a face, but lately the only name and face that filled her thoughts was back in Monaco. It was truly beginning to irritate her.

Anika was greeted with smiles, even from her mother, who seemed to approve of her appearance for once.

She smiled and made small talk, wondering when the woman would show up so they could finally order. Anika sipped her water and took a slice of the bread from the table. If she didn't show up soon, she couldn't promise that there would be any left for her.

It was heavenly, or it could have been, because she was half starved. She quickly finished it off and reached for another.

"Sorry I'm late."

Anika froze. There was no mistaking the owner of that voice.

The bread fell from her nerveless fingers as she turned along with everyone else to greet the newcomer. Only she didn't want to greet him. She wanted to throw the bread at him. Scream at him. Run to him.

Kiss him.

But she could only stay rooted to her seat and stare while everyone else got to their feet to welcome him.

Luca looked good—too good. In his usual black suit and white shirt, he wore a tie as well this time. Anika flexed her fingers as they itched to reach up and tug it off. As he got closer, her breath caught when she realized it was one of the ties he had wanted to use on her during their first encounter. She shifted in her seat, trying to mitigate any friction against the throbbing between her thighs.

He greeted everyone in turn but his attention stayed on Anika. Luca's dark eyes held hers and she couldn't look away. Breathless and more than a little panicked, she watched him, completely mesmerized by the way he dominated the room. The way he watched her with absolute focus.

"Anika?"

"Hmm?" She wasn't sure who had spoken to her. But a tap on her shoulder broke their eye contact.

Her father smiled. "Have you and Luca met?"

If her father knew, he wouldn't have been so calm.

"We met all too briefly in Monaco," Luca provided helpfully. He took her hand and brushed his lips over her knuckles. "It's a pleasure to see you again."

What could she do? If she ran out as she wanted to do, it would just raise questions. But would she be able to sit through an entire meal with him without losing it completely?

Luca pulled out her seat for her, and she poured herself into it while he took the one next to her.

"So you two met in Monaco? What a coincidence!" Isabella beamed at them. "Did you spend much time together?"

All the time they had spent together flashed through Anika's mind.

Luca smiled a little. "We were both there alone, so I cajoled her into having a couple of meals with me. We also visited the casino and the opera."

Did he have to mention the opera? Anika's head swam. "Do you mind if we order?"

"Of course not." Luca immediately caught the attention of a waiter and waved him over before putting his hand gently on her arm. "Are you okay?"

Not in the least. "Fine." Heat from his touch blasted up from his slight contact. She tugged her arm out of reach under the guise of taking a sip of her water. She kept her hand clutched on it like a lifeline well out of his way. How could she possibly be okay?

Apparently, the rest of his team were simply placeholders for him. Once Luca placed his order, the rest of them discreetly made excuses and disappeared from the restaurant.

Anika's mother didn't seem phased and watched them with great interest. "So, Luca. How long are you going to be in London?"

His thigh grazed Anika's.

He smiled mildly. "That depends on how this meeting goes."

She gripped the table but quickly released it in the hopes that no one had noticed. One look at Luca told her he had.

And it infuriated her. "It's nice of you to take time out of your busy schedule to come see us. Your time is taken up with a great many things, so I'm surprised you were able to tear yourself away."

He gazed at her levelly, refusing to take the bait. "I heard wonderful things about the De Winter Group. I just want to see it live on."

"So you decided to flash your cash in a humanitarian effort? I'm sure your team's told you that we're doing fine. We don't need your help."

"Anika…" Her father looked mildly alarmed now.

Isabella put her hand on her husband's arm. "Anika has been going through a rough time of late. I'm not sure if you've heard, but we wouldn't have taken up your time unless it was warranted."

Anika had had enough. If he wanted to come charging in like a white knight he could go right ahead. She knew what he truly was. "You should iron out the details with them." She slid out of her seat and nodded to her parents before giving Luca a parting glare. "Mother, Father. Luca."

Luca wasn't going to let her walk out on him again. Giving her parents an apologetic glance, he took off after her.

He hadn't slept since she'd left. Knowing she would be incensed by what she saw in Monaco, he'd thought he'd offer an olive branch. Helping the De Winter Group seemed like a good idea at the time. Now, however…

He chased her through the restaurant and out into the night. "Anika, wait!"

"Stay away from me, Luca!"

He caught up with her as she handed her ticket to the valet. He closed his hand around her wrist and could feel her rapid pulse fluttering against his thumb. Added to the pallid tone of her skin and wide, blank stare, it sent chills skittering down his spine. "Anika, please. Let me explain."

"I can't do this right now, Luca."

"Then tell me when you *can* talk. I'll be there." He meant it, though he'd rather hash things out with her now. Before she worried herself ill. She didn't look very well as it was and it had only been a couple of days. What would she look like in a few more?

It wasn't something he wanted to find out.

She stared at him for a long moment. Then she stumbled.

Luca's heart plummeted as he caught her by the waist to steady her.

She shoved at him. "I'm fine."

"Like hell you are." He held her until the valet returned with the Ferrari she'd told him about in Monaco. Luca ushered her into the passenger seat before climbing in behind the wheel. "Where do you live?"

"It'll be easier if I just drive."

"You're in no condition to drive. Now are you going to tell me or am I going to have to go and ask your parents?"

Damn. Her parents. They'd just left them there. He would explain later. He had more important things to deal with.

"Are you always this bossy?"

She tried to glare at him but couldn't muster the energy, which only made his heart beat faster.

Only when he was terrified. "Just give me directions." Blood rushing in his ears, he started the engine and pulled away from the curb.

It took them a while to get through the city traffic, during which he kept looking over at Anika to make sure she was okay. She stared stubbornly out of the window, only speaking to tell him when to turn. Some of her paleness had faded, but only because anger had heightened the color on her cheeks.

At least that was something.

She directed him to a new, nice-looking building and pointed him toward the parking garage. A quick swipe of her fob and they were in. A few more minutes and they walked through the door of her apartment.

He helped her onto her couch and knelt in front of her. "When was the last time you ate?"

"I had coffee…throughout the day." She rubbed her temples. "And grapes…and bread at the restaurant."

Luca got up and spun, surveying around her space.

"What are you doing?"

He spotted it and started walking before he'd stopped spinning. "Looking for your kitchen."

Anika got to her feet but froze when he turned to level his gaze at her.

"Sit. Let me take care of you."

And amazingly, she did.

He ascribed that little miracle to her being too worn out to argue. He raided her fridge and managed to put together a quick sandwich. He grabbed a bottle of water and brought it all straight to her. "What would you do without me? Eat."

"Starve, obviously," she grumbled. Despite her words, she took a big bite of the sandwich and sighed happily.

Luca swept his gaze over her. "I'd ask how you've been, but I can see that for myself."

"I'm fine. I've just been busy." She glared at him over another mouthful. "You've got me home safe, proved you're a good guy. You can leave now."

"Not until we've talked."

She glowered at him over the sandwich. "You said I could give you a time and a place."

"Better than now?" He sat on the chair in front of her. "Please, just listen.

"You can talk but I can't guarantee I'll listen." She took a swig of the water and sat back. Waiting.

Luca wasn't going to pass up the chance. What was the best way to start? He got up and strode the length of the room, turned on his heel and paced back to where he started. He did it twice more as he put his thoughts together. He'd made presentations before and they were child's play compared to this. "There is a lot about myself that you don't know. That you should know, because...because I lo—"

A strange sound stopped him mid-sentence. He spun to face her and groaned. It turned into a half chuckle when he saw her head lolled to one side. She made a snuffling sound as she settled into sleep. Of all the times for her to fall asleep. Still, he was grateful for it.

Anika looked as though she hadn't slept in days. Which he could completely understand, he hadn't slept since she'd left either. He had felt as though he'd lost a part of himself. He'd been itching to see her again and had been trying to figure out the best way. Unfortunately, it seemed that there was no good way to approach Anika. So he went for speed over anything else. The last thing he needed was for her to have time to talk herself out of feeling anything for him.

Luca watched her for a moment, enjoying her relaxed features. He hated seeing her so anxious and angry. Things had to be set straight and soon.

He cradled her in his arms and walked down the corridor until he found her room. Figuring she would be livid if she found he'd undressed her, he took off her shoes and covered her with the blanket.

After a few seconds of his conscience wrestling with his libido, better judgment won. Luca took a pillow and walked out to the living room. The couch was plenty big enough for him to sleep on, though he'd much rather be in bed with her. Not that he'd get much sleep anyway.

He took off his jacket, flopped onto the plush sofa and thumped the pillow a few times to try to find some comfort.

At least she hadn't kicked him out.

* * * *

Anika jerked awake at the insistent buzzing of the intercom on her wall. What the hell? She looked down at herself. Still fully dressed and in bed. Heart pounding in her throat, she froze for a second.

Luca?

She remembered the restaurant and him driving her home, but not much else. Instinctively, running her fingers through her hair and over her rumpled clothing, she dashed to the intercom and hit the button to activate the video, but whoever it was had rung off.

Maybe they'd called the wrong apartment?

Anika shrugged. She was more interested in Luca and where he was.

She quietly padded into the living room to find him at the door, speaking quietly to someone.

The man on the other side wasn't one she wanted to see. "Joshua? What are you doing here?"

He looked pleadingly at her from under the barricade of Luca's arm. "I need to talk to you, Anika."

She stayed where she was. "I think you said enough when you didn't show up for our wedding. Thanks for that, by the way."

"That's what I want to talk to you about. I need to apologize." He looked at Luca. "I'd rather not do it like this."

"There's nothing to be said, Josh."

"Can I just come in?" He peeked at Luca again. "Did you hire security? Are you in danger?"

That thought seemed to give him pause. Anika almost went along with it just to get rid of him, but it wouldn't have been fair. She shook her head. "Joshua Rhys-Jones, meet Luca Rossi."

Joshua narrowed his eyes. "I've heard of you." His gaze ping-ponged between them. "What's he doing here?"

Luca smiled sleepily and let the door close, crossing the room to stand next to her. "Anika and I were having a business dinner last night and she wasn't feeling well so I drove her home."

"So you decided to stay the night? How very gallant of you." Joshua's shoulders went rigid. "Well I'm here now, so you can go."

"You're kidding, right?" All fatigue blasted from her system, leaving only boiling anger. "Have you said everything you wanted to? Because I've had enough."

He put up his hands, still watching Luca. "I know I have no right to come barging in here and breaking up whatever this" — he waved his hand at them — "is. But I wanted to apologize for what happened and I want to try again."

"Now I really know you're joking." She scrubbed her hand over her face. "What makes you think I would ever want to try that again?"

"Because it's in the best interest of our families?"

Anika couldn't believe what she was hearing. After getting a taste of what Luca had to offer, she had no intention of ever getting back together with Joshua. She deserved someone who actually cared about her. Someone who she cared about. Not some hollow, fake relationship. "I don't think so."

"Perhaps you should find yourself some new investors?" Luca chimed in.

Anika glared at him before turning back to Joshua. "It would never work, Josh. Sorry."

Joshua took a step forward, and Luca immediately crowded him. Watching them, she couldn't imagine how she would have been happy with Joshua. They were polar opposites, at least as far as coloring. Though both were handsome, Joshua didn't have the presence Luca did. He seemed to shrink away simply being in the same room as Luca. And while she couldn't judge her ex-fiancé on a few things, she doubted he would match up to Luca in any way.

But Joshua had been honest when he hadn't turned up for their wedding. Luca had barely waited for her to come back from the ladies' room to make a move on someone else.

The memory was like an ice pick through the heart.

Joshua looked at Luca before trying to tug Anika aside. She jerked her arm out of his reach before he got very far. Joshua launched into his spiel then. "I think we can make it work. I was just a little panicked. It wasn't how I thought I would meet the woman I'd marry and I got cold feet."

Anika had heard enough. "Thank you for being a coward. If you hadn't we'd have spent the rest of our lives miserable. So thanks, but I don't want to see you again."

Joshua's face fell. "But, Anika…"

"That's all I have to say about it."

He clenched his jaw. "So what's going on with you and this guy? Did you meet him in Monaco? Or was it something that was ongoing from before? Do you love him?"

The last question echoed in her mind. "I don't have to tell you anything, Joshua. Please leave."

"I'm right, aren't I? You were just using me for my family's money. You're with this guy, aren't you? That's why you wouldn't sleep with me!" He ran his gaze over Luca and sneered. "You know the stories about him, right? How could you not? The whole world knows about his ways. He'll use you and cast you aside without a moment's regret, Anika."

As if she needed to be told that. The memory of seeing him with the blonde had been permanently burned into her brain.

"That's enough!" Luca stepped even closer and looked down his nose at Joshua, using his superior size to intimidate. "Anika asked you to leave."

"I don't have to listen to you." He paled the instant the words were out of his mouth. Luca was bigger than he was and definitely more intimidating. "It just so happens I *do* have places to be." He gave Anika one last look. "Don't be stupid and fall for him."

Too late.

Luca held the door open for him and watched him walk out with a satisfied smirk on his face.

"Don't look too pleased with yourself. You might as well ask him to hold the elevator."

The smile died. "Anika. Will you let me explain?"

"About what? That you couldn't keep your hands off another woman for five seconds while I was worrying about—everything?" Anika stared daggers at him. "You couldn't even bring yourself to ask her to leave. You were the one who wanted to meet in the first place."

He crossed the room over to her in a flash. "I wanted her to leave. I asked her to leave. But she got it into her head that she wants me."

Anika stalked toward the door, her hand tight on the handle. "I can't imagine why. When I saw you two last, she was practically in your lap."

She could see he was trying to keep calm. "Anika. That was because that pink-haired blogger who has been plaguing us both was there!"

"What?" She instantly deflated. "How did she find us?"

"I don't know." Luca took her hands and attempted to pull her toward the couch. When she resisted, he stopped but continued to hold her hands as if he couldn't bring himself to let go. "She was the one who sent Chantelle over. She wanted pictures to go with yet another article about me it seemed."

"How do you know?" She gripped his hands.

He looked a bit more hopeful that she hadn't made him let go and dove into the story. "Chantelle told me. She isn't one to keep quiet about much. After I spotted the pink-haired menace, I played along, hoping she would focus on me so you could get out of there." He stroked the backs of her hands with his thumbs. "I know how much you hate being in the tabloids."

He had done that for her?

She knew he didn't care what people thought of him, but Luca wasn't the type of man to let himself take the fall for anyone. He heart bobbed in her chest a little.

"You look confused." He ran his thumb down her cheek. "Let's sit."

Anika nodded, but she still needed a little space. She couldn't think straight when he touched her. He had diverted attention from her so she could avoid embarrassment? The blonde meant nothing to him? Her heart fluttered. Did he truly care for her? Or was he more devious? Did he think he could get a slice of DWG through her? Her mind reeled at the thought. She didn't want to believe that, but he had sent a team to meet with her parents. Could he be that cruel?

She edged toward the kitchen. "Can I get you something to eat? I'm still hungry and I haven't seen you eat a thing, either."

Concern etched his face. "Don't worry about me."

He did, however, follow her into the kitchen.

"You can sit, you know." Anika couldn't get enough space between them to stop her body from reacting. She needed to think.

Luca stayed an arm's reach away. "I won't be a bother."

And he wasn't. In fact, he actually helped her put together a couple of sandwiches adding a few touches here and there.

So he knew how to make sandwiches too. "Last night's sandwich wasn't a fluke, then?"

"I'm sure I could surprise you with a few skills I possess." He winked at her, took the plates and let her lead the way back to the table.

The suggestiveness of his comment lit an ember in Anika. He'd continued to surprise her more and more each time they were together.

When they sat, as hungry as she was, she found herself more interested in the man next to her and his intentions. "Why are you here, Luca?"

He sighed. "Because I couldn't stay away. I had planned to wait a few days. Letting you come to me, but I couldn't take the chance that you might not. I didn't want you to have the option to forget me."

"How could I ever forget you?" He'd been on her mind from the moment she'd met him. After their weekend together Anika would remember him for the rest of her life. "Would it be so easy for you to forget me?"

Luca stared at her incredulously "Of course not! I have thought of nothing but you since we met!"

That put a smile on her face. When he kissed her knuckles, her smile grew even more.

"But there are some things you need to know about me."

The growing euphoria dimmed a little. "Like what?"

He truly did want a controlling stake in her family's company? He was involved with someone else? Married? Had ties to some unsavory people? Was that where his money came from? Anika clamped down on her rampant imagination. The long pause before he spoke twisted her gut.

His voice was soft when he finally spoke. "Remember when you asked me about how I met René in Nice?"

She nodded. Anika could recall every second of that trip.

"Years ago, René supported his family with a little cart on the waterfront. He'd wheel it up and down selling socca. Became well known for it. But his fame also made him a target because he made so much money over the day."

She didn't like where this was going. "He was attacked?"

"Many times I'm sure. But late one summer night, he was ambushed by a group of kids. Hungry street kids looking for a little cash. Maybe a little something to eat. He fought them off with the aid of a few tourists who heard him call for help."

That was a relief. "You were one of the tourists?"

His eyes stayed trained on the sandwiches. "I was one of the kids."

Anika's stomach dropped. She couldn't have heard him right. "But he's so friendly with you. Surely, he wouldn't be with someone who tried to rob him."

"I should probably start at the beginning." His grip tightened infinitesimally before releasing again. "I haven't always been Luca Rossi. I was born Antonio Luca Luchesi. If you look up that name, I'm sure you'll find it attached to all kinds of petty crime that I had been engaged in as a child."

It was as though her brain had slipped a gear. Her mind spun and spun but just couldn't get back on track. "I don't understand." Though it made some sense since the search she made on him came up with nothing before his success.

"I changed it, obviously. Partially because I wanted to distance myself from the boy I was, but mostly because I had been named after a man I despised." Luca took a slow breath. "My father wasn't a nice man. He wasn't a good man. Not successful. He was nothing, really. He'd gotten my mother pregnant while they were teens. And he resented her for forcing a family on him that he never wanted and me for being born. He drank heavily, beat us regularly. My childhood wasn't something I would wish on anyone."

"Oh, Luca…"

He shook his head. "One night when I was twelve, I begged my mother to run away with me, but she refused. I think she remembered a part of him that she wanted to come back and probably hoped it would one day. I couldn't stand staying any longer. I didn't care what he did to me, but I couldn't watch him hurt her anymore."

Luca's eyes turned bleak. "It wasn't anything new. I'd begged her before, but this time he heard me. He'd come home early from a day of drinking and gambling. Laughed at me. Told me even if I did get away I would amount to nothing. That I would die in the gutter. And he beat me to within an inch of my life. Mama defended me. Got in his way and, as he raged, he pushed her down the stairs. She was a tiny woman. He only had to throw his arm out and she flew. I still remember the sound of her scream, the silence when she came to a stop and lay crumpled at the bottom. Of course, he blamed me and came after me with a knife. I was sure he would kill me that time, so I ran."

Anika cupped her hands over his pale cheeks, not that he seemed to notice. He was so caught up in his memories he looked like the lost little boy he described. Heart aching, she turned his face up to look at her.

"That's why you were so angry at the thought of me not having our baby if I am pregnant?"

Luca nodded jerkily. "I promised myself many things long ago." He counted off on his fingers. "I would be in control of my destiny. I would become a success. I would never become like my father. I would never love like my mother. And if I ever had a child, he or she would know their father and would want for nothing."

Her heart melted.

"Anyway, I lived on the streets for a while. Learned how to survive the hard way. Eventually, I hopped a train and somehow made it to Nice. There were stories about the money that flowed there. How generous tourists were." He smiled softly. "To be honest, I just wanted to be near the water. Once there, I got mixed up with a bunch of homeless kids. We ended up getting involved in some stupid things. Dangerous things."

And that was why he'd been so angry about her falling asleep on the beach. He knew what dangers were out there. He'd experienced it. He had worried about her.

Luca laughed humorlessly. "I'd been there almost a month that night we tried to rob René, and I was the only one caught. René must have seen something in me that he liked because he took me in. Gave me a home and a job. Said whatever I earned in tips was mine."

Anika could only imagine the tips that his handsome face got him, as he grew older. "I bet you made a killing."

He chuckled. "I learned at a young age that a pretty face can get you almost anything you want. I worked my ass off for René. Saved up everything I made. Learned everything I could. How to clean. How to cook. Languages. Business. Everything. Up until then, he'd been the only father I'd truly had. He kept me in line, taught me a lot. Kicked my ass when I needed it, something he had to do often. I changed my name when I got older. My mother always called me Luca and I took her last name." He shrugged. "I've been Luca Rossi ever since."

Enthralled, Anika asked, "Did you buy that restaurant for René?"

The smile on his face answered that for her, but he nodded.

"I wanted to buy him a bigger one once I'd made my first million, but he laughed and said he had everything he ever wanted and needed. He was my inspiration to do what I do. I find people with good ideas and help expand on them."

And he was obviously very good at finding the right people. He certainly didn't want for much.

Luca looked at her then, his expression a little apprehensive. "I spent the next decade or so of my life amassing my fortune, helping others and not much else. It wasn't until I met you that things changed."

"Things, meaning…?"

"Meaning you slowly changed my view of relationships."

Anika smiled. "That makes two of us."

Luca bumped his forehead to hers. "So. Now that you know all that, what do you think of me?"

With the pieces of the Luca puzzle in place, it only strengthened her feelings for him. Anika knew she loved the man before. She could deny it all she wanted, but now her heart burst with it. He'd suffered and overcame so much in his life. It was a miracle they'd even found each another. A simple twist here or there in the story and they would never have met.

Anika nibbled her bottom lip. "Why are you telling me this now?"

Luca chuckled softly and pecked her on the nose. "Haven't you guessed? I would have thought someone with a mind as agile as yours would have figured out my intent by now."

Anika drew back to look him in the eyes. She could see everything there. Admiration. Shame. Apprehension. Love. They shone through unfettered. He was there—all of him—for her judgment.

She smiled broadly. "Sometimes when a girl is in love with someone she likes to hear it from him first. You know, just to be sure she's not the only one."

Luca's posture relaxed, sagging a little with relief. He tugged her over so she sat cradled in his lap. "Anika, I love you. More than I ever thought I could love anyone. I know I'm not perfect—far from it—but I will never let you down. I'd die before I'd let that happen." He pulled out a little box and flicked it open to reveal a beautiful ring. The stone was tasteful, a perfect diamond, not overly large, set in a band of delicate vines to wind around her finger. One vine on either side was a string of tiny diamonds that joined the others to hold the eye-catching main stone. "I noticed that your jewelry is all set in platinum so I had a team at De Winter create this from a design I had in mind. If it's not what you want, I can have another made in whatever style you like."

"The man designs rings as well." Grinning, she held out her hand. "Are you going to stop talking and ask me properly?"

He took her hand but didn't budge from where he was. Their relationship had been anything but regular so why should this be?

"Anika? Will you be my wife and make me happier than any other man on the planet?"

She didn't have to think about it. "Yes!"

Luca kissed her knuckle just above where the ring would sit before taking it out of the box and slipping it onto her finger.

Anika took a moment to admire the ring before winding her arms around his neck. "It's perfect. *You're* perfect."

"Only trying to match you." He kissed her like a man starved. "I've missed you so much."

"Me too." She pulled him closer, dragged him down over her.

Luca obliged. Sliding out from under her to lay on his side on the expansive couch, he kept his legs entwined with hers. "I thought you were hungry."

Food could wait. She had only one concern and that was Luca. Anika went to work on his shirt, unbuttoning as fast as she could make her fingers go. "Later."

He laughed. "I like the way you think." Luca's nimble fingers made fast work of her dress and bra.

Anika nearly purred when he cupped her breasts. "I've missed those hands."

He smiled mischievously at her. "Just my hands?" Luca ground himself against her, smiling when she arched into him.

"Maybe not just your hands," she gasped.

"Good." Hitching an arm under her, he bent her bowed him so her breasts raised perfectly aligned for his lips.

Anika's eyes rolled back when the wet heat of his mouth closed around her peaked nipple. She sighed when he curled his tongue around it and he sucked. Meanwhile, he skimmed his hand downward to the waistband of her panties, tracing the edge before pulling them down and shoving the offending article of clothing down her legs.

Job done, he caressed his way back up her leg, pausing a moment to run his thumb reverently over her hipbone before slipping it into her panties. The gentle touch of him on her sensitized clit had her rearing up against him, seeking more of Luca.

He easily eased two fingers into her and crooked them slowly, teasingly. Rocking her hips against him, she tried to get him to speed up, go deeper, but he wouldn't be deterred. "Luca! You're driving me crazy!"

"That's the idea."

He nipped her bottom lip, adding to her frustration.

Anika's mind blanked. Instinctively, she sought to get his clothes off. It didn't matter how. It just mattered that she did. Abandoning the buttons on his shirt, she slid her hands up under the hem, seeking the hot taut skin of his rippling abdomen. The belt of his trousers only frustrated her more, so she went straight for the zipper, undoing it and pushing her hand through to curl around his straining erection through his briefs. She'd see how long he'd take being teased.

Luca groaned her name, letting her do as she pleased for a moment before he tore her hand away and pinned it above her head. "Keep that up and this will be over far too soon."

The comment she had ready died in her throat when Luca rocked his hand purposefully, putting just the right amount of pressure on her clit, pumping his fingers inside her with clear intent. Anika had no complaints as her body wound tighter and tighter until she arched under him, her head falling back with a cry.

When she could get her eyes to open and focus, Anika found herself staring up at Luca's smugly self-satisfied face.

"Your bed?"

Anika took a second to process the request. She was so focused on getting him naked she didn't really care where they were.

He kissed her gently. "I want to do this right and making love to my fiancée on her couch doesn't seem fitting for the occasion."

Chuckling, she relented. "Come on, then. But I expect you naked by the time we get there."

"Yes, dear." He'd already started on his clothes.

She swiped her hand against his now naked butt. "None of that." Anika took a few steps forward and paused to get a look at her soon-to-be husband as he kicked the trousers off and shucked his shirt behind her. She couldn't imagine a more handsome man. Tall, dark-haired, tan skin, broad-shouldered, chiseled body, long muscular legs, and very virile, he was the perfect male specimen.

And he was all hers.

She grabbed his hand the moment he was free of his clothing and dragged him behind her down the hall to her bedroom.

Anika shoved him onto the bed and climbed on over him to come to a stop straddling his midsection and pinning his arms down with her knees. How would he like the tables turned on him? Anika knew if he wanted, he could easily lift her off, but for the moment, he seemed more than content to play along.

She reached behind her to stroke him, loving the way he strained at her touch. She teased him with light fingers and sweeping motions.

"Anika..." The warning tone in his voice only spurred her on.

As she smiled sweetly down at him, she stretched farther to cup his balls. "Yes?"

He ground out words that sounded like an oath as he picked her up and rolled her under him. Luca adjusted himself, notching the head of his erection, when he jerked back, with a groan.

Anika froze. "What's wrong?"

"I don't have a condom. They're in my trousers."

He eased off her, obviously about to get them.

She clutched at his shoulders halting his movements. "Wait."

Luca gazed down at her, studying her for a long while. "What are you saying?"

Anika tried to gauge his reaction, but couldn't go beyond what she was feeling. "I spent the past few days agonizing over whether or not I'm pregnant. I even bought the tests yesterday." At his hopeful look, she shook her head. "I haven't taken them yet. It's still too early to tell. But I've found myself leaning toward wanting a positive result. I know it's really soon but... What do you think?" She looked up at him.

A smile grew over his face. The smile he gave her was one of awe and happiness.

"You know I can't say no to you. Especially when your wishes align with my own." Luca kissed her softly. "You're sure?"

"Absolutely."

He reverently ran his fingers over her cheek as he kissed her. Luca scooped his arm around her, levering her up into him so that every inch of their bodies touched.

Anika wound herself around his big body, unwilling to let any space come between them. She'd never been so terrified or exhilarated at the same time but she knew if she were with Luca, everything would work out fine. More than fine.

He kissed her as if he hadn't seen her in months and he wanted to remember what she tasted like. What it was like to kiss her. One second it was deep and penetrating, his tongue tangling with hers. The next soft and sweeping, tantalizing. He kissed her on the lips, the neck, her collarbone, her breasts. His mouth and tongue explored, tasted, teased.

Luca made his way slowly down her body, his hands and mouth blazing a trail over her ribs to press a deferential kiss on her lower stomach. His gaze met hers as he shifted down, hitching her legs over his broad shoulders.

Then he kissed her *there*. The gentle press of his lips soon turned into hot open-mouthed caresses as he devoured her.

Her orgasm caught her off guard. Hard and fast, it hit, curling her toes and bowing her under him with a cry as sparks burst behind her eyelids.

He didn't give her a chance to recover. Luca slid up over her. He reached between them to adjust himself, thrusting deep the instant he found her slit. He stared down into her eyes holding her gaze as he moved, his eyes black and hypnotic, peering deep into hers. His thick erection plunged, dragging past sensitized flesh, while he rubbed his thumb in small circles over her clit, sending waves of sensation rolling through her, each one building on the last.

He thrust deeper and deeper, his eyes never leaving hers. Anika held his gaze until the first cresting wave of her orgasm overtook her. Luca lowered his head to the hollow of her neck as his pace quickened. It had always been good between them, but never like this. It was as though their entire beings were merging in that moment.

Luca collapsed onto her and for a moment, they lay entwined fighting to catch their breaths. He rolled to the side with a grunt and for a long while simply stared at her as he recovered.

Anika stared right back unabashedly studying his handsome face. "I have some things to confess too."

"Oh, yeah?" He turned on his side and propped his head up with his hand, his smile teasing. "And you waited until after you'd taken advantage of me, huh?"

"Yep." She turned to mirror his posture. "I hadn't planned on coming to Monaco. My friend talked me into it. Told me she had it all arranged. It wasn't until I arrived that I found out her claim was slightly exaggerated. She had bumped your...friend...as a favor to me."

He digested the information with a small shrug. "I can't say I approve of her methods, but as it turned out to our advantage, I can't complain."

"She'll never let me forget this, you know. She's going to be insufferable. All our lives Petra's been coming up with schemes, and for the first time, it's worked out. In any capacity."

His lips tilted in a lopsided smile. "Petra Bauer?"

Anika's eyes widened when she realized what she'd given away. "Don't tell anyone. I don't want her to get into trouble."

"I doubt she would. James...Conroy," he clarified, "has a soft spot for her. He might not like what she did, but he won't be too concerned over that. But don't worry, he won't find out from me."

Anika pecked him on the mouth. "Thank you."

"Anything for you."

Feeling blessed, Anika snuggled up to him. Running her hands up his stomach, she chuckled at his groan when she trailed her hand downward.

"You're going to be the death of me, woman." Even though he grumbled, Luca wrapped his arms around her, rolling her on top of him where she could feel his renewing desire.

"I hope not, because we've got time to make up for." Hitching her legs on either side of him, she had his hardening erection pinned between them as she rocked against him.

He ran his hands up her sides and down again to rest on her hips. Luca seemed perfectly content to her let do as she pleased as he watched her. He gazed up at her, his eyes half lidded as she slid back and forth over him.

As he hardened, the friction grew more and more pleasurable. Anika lifted herself up to angle him enough to slide onto. Rocking experimentally, she slowly found an angle and rhythm that worked for them both.

Gratification flooded through her as she learned how to move her body to bring them both pleasure. When her impending orgasm made her rhythm erratic, Luca took over. He gripped her hips and thrust up into her, seeking to reach the same goal. It took seconds for her to climax and he followed close behind with a shout.

Luca pulled her down to his chest and held her close, as she lay sprawled over him. Anika pressed her hand over his heart while she listened to the beat slow and become steady. He toyed with the ring on her finger as he held her securely with his other arm. Anika couldn't think of a time she was more content.

Smiling against his chest, she closed her eyes, happier than she'd ever been.

Epilogue

Two weeks later...

Anika woke up to the scent of coffee and something sweet. Waffles? It was wonderful since she was starving. "Luca?"

His smiling face poked in through the door moments later. "Morning. I had hoped to get this to you before you woke." Luca presented her with a tray of food. "I hope this is okay."

"This is amazing." It was then that she noticed he was dressed. The dark suit looked fantastic on him, though she would have been happier to see him in nothing at all. "Going somewhere?"

"I have a meeting then four more. There's a lot of work involved moving my operation here." Luca's gaze wandered over her and his smile grew regretful. "Though I sorely wish I could just drop it on someone else's shoulders at the moment."

Speaking of work. Anika lurched for her phone. "What time is it?"

"Time enough for us to have a quick bite." He blocked her escape from the bed, tore off a piece of waffle and stuffed it into her mouth. "You need to have a little something at least." He shoved a bit of waffle into his own mouth and chewed.

Anika shook her head in mock exasperation. It was nice to have someone taking care of her, though it was hardly needed. "I've been looking out for myself for a long time, Luca."

"Well now you have me to help." He planted a kiss on her head. "What have you got on your plate today?"

As far as she was concerned, she could take on anything. "I have a bunch of meetings. My parents want us to join them for dinner."

Luca nodded. "Sounds like fun."

"Doesn't it just?" She groaned and flopped back on the pillows. "Wouldn't it be wonderful to fly back to Monaco and just forget the rest of the world existed?"

"If only we could. We should go back. Soon."

"Promise me we will."

"Whenever you want."

Smiling up at him, Anika sighed. She liked that he didn't assume that she would quit her job, her life, now they were together. She was marrying a billionaire, after all. Anika never had to work again if she didn't want to. Not that she had to now. But it made her feel as though she had done something with her life. Unlike the celebutantes she'd been acquainted with who frittered away their lives partying and grabbing headlines with who they were sleeping with next or wardrobe malfunctions. The day might come, one day, where she wouldn't want to work any longer. Perhaps once they had kids. She hated growing up with a string of nannies and barely ever seeing her parents. Anika swore she would be a different type of parent. And she would be.

Her hand drifted to her middle. How soon would that be?

"Daydreaming?" His hand closed over hers, warm and comforting, as he peered into her eyes.

"Maybe."

Luca brought her hand to his lips. "Perhaps it's time to try out those tests?"

Her mind blanked. As excited as she was to find out for sure, Anika couldn't make herself move. What if she was? What if she wasn't? Her heart fluttered while the rest of her was petrified.

His expression clouded. "If you'd rather wait…"

Anika took a deep breath. "Just working up the courage."

Luca dropped onto the bed next to her and wrapped his arms around her. "No matter the result, it doesn't change how I feel about you."

She knew that already, but hearing it definitely bolstered her courage somewhat. "I know. It's just so huge…" Anika kissed him and slipped out of his embrace. If she didn't do it now, when would she?

The test was taken then set aside while she waited on the edge of the tub, tapping out a nervous tattoo on her legs. As freaked out as she was, with every passing second, Anika's conviction for what she wanted the result to be grew.

There were about thirty-four and a half seconds left to go when she looked and saw the result. After about a minute of staring at the test, she opened the door.

Her dazed expression was enough to stop his pacing when she walked back into the bedroom.

He crossed the space in a few quick steps to take her hands once again. "Well?"

Anika brought his hands to her stomach. "As the mother of your child, I don't think it would be too much to ask you to take those clothes off, get back in bed with me and make sure we celebrate thoroughly before we go to work."

Luca's jaw hung loose for a long moment before a huge grin spread over his face. His hands curved over her belly as if he was searching for proof. "Truly?"

Anika nodded then let out a squeal of delight when he picked her up and swung her around.

He reverently laid her on the bed then impatiently tore off his clothes. Luca kissed his way up her legs, stopping at her belly to give it a gentle caress of his mouth on his way up to taste her lips.

When he drew back, Anika was breathless as she looked up at him. "Are we completely insane? We've known each other only a few weeks and we're engaged, expecting a baby, and dreaming about happily ever after."

"I don't think so." He kissed her, long and lingering. "We are people who know our own minds. What we want. And we—" He kissed her again. "Belong together. We both know it. Otherwise, neither of us would be here. Besides, we're both stubborn enough to make the future what we want it to be."

She smiled. "So what happens now?"

His smile grew wicked. "First we're going to call in and delegate our work for the next couple of days so we can celebrate properly, then I'm going to make love to you until neither of us can move. After that, we're going to get married and live happily ever after."

Anika hooked her arms around Luca and dragged him closer. "Sounds good to me."

About the Author

Kait was born and raised in the wilderness of the Pacific Northwest and started writing as a child to entertain herself during the long winters. Insatiably curious with a love of learning new things, she's picked up many random skills including three languages and two martial arts. After traveling three continents (the other four are on her bucket list), she settled in England with her family where she spends most of her time cultivating her daughter's love of reading and writing, scribbling ideas on every available scrap of paper and trying out dialog on her cat.

Kait Gamble loves to hear from readers. You can find her contact information, website and author biography at http://www.totallybound.com.

Home of Erotic Romance